Praise for *Hystera*:

"*Hystera* is a haunting, mesmerizing story of madness, longing and identity, set against one of the most fascinating times in NYC history. Skolkin-Smith's alchemy is to inhabit her characters even as she crafts a riveting story that is nothing short of brilliant."
— Caroline Leavitt, *New York Times* bestselling author of *Pictures of You*

"In language with the wild power of accuracy, *Hystera* maps a path through the landscape of trauma and illness, the feverish news of the seventies, and a character's own indelibly vivid imagery of alarm and comfort. An eye-opening novel."
— Joan Silber, author of *Ideas of Heaven: A Ring of Stories*, finalist for the National Book Award

"Leora Skolkin-Smith's new novel, *Hystera*, provides a very vivid sense of being in the head of someone having a psychotic breakdown, and is a powerfully useful reference book for dealing with the mental-health system. It also pungently evokes the gritty New York of the '70s."
— Robert Whitcomb, *The Providence Journal*

"Inside a psychiatric ward in the 1970s, Leora Skolkin-Smith's *Hystera* takes you on a ride through the wilderness of a young woman's emotional trauma and breakdown, and seizes upon the intricacies of mental health, our phobias, and fears around it. Brilliantly envisioned, this story of passion, and familial dysfunction, bears witness to an exquisite reknitting of a young woman's soul, told in language that is brave, startling and ultimately tender and wise."

   – Jessica Keener, author of *Night Swim*

"Leora Skolkin-Smith's novel *Hystera* is an unforgettable story of mental illness. Set in the New York City of the 1970s, the book is told in precise language that sears the characters into your consciousness."

   – Largehearted Boy

"I loved this book because it was about a writer, of course. But I also loved it because of the writing itself – the amazing techniques that can be observed – learned from – if the reader doesn't get too caught up in the forward motion of the story and the tone of the book not to pay attention."

   – Carolyn Howard-Johnson, Red Room

"One of those novels that gets you in the first few sentences; you know you are in for something completely unique and interesting in only a few seconds.... A great and interesting read for sure, and one I highly recommend."

   – Veronica MD

"Tragically beautiful."

   – Ragmag

"I highly recommend this book. The writing is outstanding and I was completely hooked from the very start until the end.... It's a short but powerful read that will stick with you and have you thinking about it long after you have finished the book."
    – Life in Review

"You can't help but be taken in with Lillian's story. I don't want to reveal too much, because I do believe that this a book you must experience for yourself."
    – A Bookish Way of Life

"Leora Skolkin-Smith has written a fascinating novel about one woman's descent into mental illness and her struggle to feel whole."
    The House of the Seven Tails

"Hystera plunges me into Lilly's world, lets me see it through her eyes, let's me become Lilly and look at a world I'm not familiar with. It left me thinking of Lilly. Days later, I can't get her out of my head."
    – Terry Marshall Fiction

Winner: Global E-book Awards
Finalist: International Book Awards, Indie Excellence Awards

HYSTERA

HYSTERA

Leora Skolkin-Smith

THE
STORY PLANT

The Story Plant
Studio Digital CT, LLC
P.O. Box 4331
Stamford, CT 06907

Jacket design by Lou Robinson

Print ISBN-13: 978-1-61188-090-8
E-book ISBN-13: 978-1-61188-091-5

Visit our website at www.TheStoryPlant.com
Visit the author's website at www.LeoraSkolkinSmith.com

First Fiction Studio printing: November 2011
First Story Plant printing: September 2013

Printed in the United States of America

For Matthew, my light always.

This book would not have come into being without the help of friends and family. I would like to thank Caroline Leavitt, Dr. Mervyn Peskin, Iris and David, Grace Paley, Danielle Durkin, the wonderful writers at Hamilton Stone Editions who read an early draft and made suggestions, and so many friends through the years who gave it and me the gift of their support and faith.

HYSTERA: from the Greek root *Hysteria*, meaning "the wandering uterus." Hippocrates viewed the womb as an independent creature. Unnatural behavior would drive the uterus to distraction and cause it to wander freely throughout the body. There were various consequences to these travels depending on how far the uterus wandered and where it chose to attach itself, but when the roving organ ultimately came to rest next to the brain, it caused hysteria.

At the end of the nineteenth century, women with hysteria were thought to suffer bodily paroxysms called *Globus hysterics* (*Globus*, from the Latin meaning "globe" or "sphere").

"...hither and thither in the flanks hystera, the women's womb, wanders, and, in a word, it is altogether erratic, on the whole the womb is like an animal within an animal."

—Paraphrased from the original Hippocratic Corpus, written in the fifth century BC

Chapter One

Inside the locked ward on Payne Whitney's fifth floor, Lilly stepped onto a steel platform. The examination room was harshly lit, the bulbs behind plastic squares on the ceiling, fluorescent and burning. The metal examining table sparked from too many electric darts and moonbeams.

It was an April evening in 1974. *The city's night lights streaming in from the window would have been enough to illuminate the room*, Lilly thought. The arrows of the moon pierced her blue-jeaned legs.

"You're a dark girl," the nurse said. "You look a little like Patty Hearst. Lillian, is that your name?"

Lilly nodded, staring up at the large woman who confused her. The nurse fisted her hands, big as a serviceman's, glossy nail polish shining on her nails, reddish-brown like her long hair. The nurse was sturdy and strong, her copious breasts bulging under a tight blue tank top.

Lilly was a mess of unbrushed hair and pale features, the odor of imported Italian sardines in olive oil on her stained T-shirt. *I want to rest now*, she wished. She turned to stare out into the darkened evening. A spring rain was slanting on the pane behind the metal bars.

"We're going to keep you here in the hospital with us a little while," the nurse said. "I'm going to examine you, Lillian. My name is Beverly."

"Examine me?"

"It's just routine. Nothing elaborate."

"That's not possible."

"I beg your pardon?"

"I can't be examined."

"Dear, all of us can be examined."

A sheet of thin white paper was pulled all the way down to the metal stirrups, attached to the base of the examining table.

"Lie down on your back now, Lillian."

Out the window, a soft indigo veiled the sky—the wind swirling, incessant. Lilly eased herself down, flat on her back. The cool air was a wet cloth slapped on Lilly's forehead. Her breathing was short, panicked.

"I need you to squish yourself down farther on the table here," Beverly said.

"Did I frighten him?" Lilly asked her.

"Who do you mean, Lillian?"

"The doctor who spoke with me in the interviewing room."

"Oh, heavens. It would take a lot to frighten Dr. Burkert."

"But is that why I'm here?"

"Howard Burkert's one of our best third-year residents. No, no. You didn't scare him. We need to know whether the pain you told him about is a physical problem, or if it's something else."

Stretched out on the examination table, Lilly wondered again if there were an abnormality in her sex, a cyst there, a tumor—maybe she was pregnant.

Her boyfriend, Mitchell, was gone.

Lilly read about body delusions. She learned, too, after her father had come home from the hospital three years ago from his long coma, the extent to which a mind could reinvent its former world, house a whole alternate universe of worlds.

Maybe Beverly and Dr. Burkert didn't know yet about her father's two cerebral strokes, his coma, his altered mind. Or his brain-damaged condition.

Five hours ago, it was freezing inside the emergency triage cubicle at New York Hospital. The winter heater must have shut down too early for April. When they took Lilly into the procedure room, they gave her a furry wool blanket and she had stopped shivering.

Let the tears in my eyes tell them a story, she thought. She practiced her story: Her father got sick; her family are strangers. Her boyfriend Mitchell left her. She would leave out the alchemical symbols of trees and phalluses that were populating her imagination with images of fire from her mother's old Hebrew texts in the basement of her parents' house. She feared the hospital staff would discover she was hallucinating the unnatural bulb between her thighs and its paroxysms—that she was really delusional. It would make them put her away. And she wanted to stay a few days in the hospital to rest, because the building was nice. *This hospital is for people recovering from unrequited love affairs*, she thought. *But the delusional cases, where were they put?* she wondered. She didn't want to find out.

Lilly remembered lying supine on the trolley in the emergency room a few hours ago, and the apparatus, like a gas mask strapped onto her nose and mouth which delivered the fumes that forced her into cloudiness. It was all she remembered about having her stomach pumped, besides the brackish-brown, sweet syrup the emergency physician handed her to drink. It made her convulse and vomit. She remembered taking the Librium pills and drinking the pint of Johnnie Walker Red two hours earlier, before her roommate, Jane, brought her to the ER.

Like a sleepwalker guided by a seeing-eye dog, she let her roommate, Jane, take her arm. Then Lilly plunged forward into a taxi, accepting Jane's warm body against hers. The whiskey felt good coursing through her system with the relief that she hadn't consummated the suicide. Yearning was a burning in her flesh. She had a love disease of flammability; love was dangerous. Intimacy made her feel as though her bowels were crying out. Everything inside her was as fragile as the web a spider spins on a tree branch in the midst of a forest fire. This is why she tried to die. She was burning up.

"Wait a minute." The nurse was looking down at her now, shaking her head. "I need to get another pair of latex gloves for this. It's going to be fine, Lillian. Please stay on the table. There's a hospital aide right outside the door. I won't be a minute."

When Lilly was alone, she looked around the sterile room. She put her hands on herself. The strange bulb was still there, nested beneath the zipper of her jeans.

₪

When Lilly first discovered the bulb, it was like a dream, but she was awake when she found it. This was a few months ago.

Late fall. Her boyfriend Mitchell was still in her life. He was making her dinner that evening. The steam from the boiling beef cubes was rank as old bologna. From the bedroom, she heard Mitchell swearing at the frying pan where the cream and butter and beer were crackling. She donned Mitchell's bathrobe and passed Jane's bowl of unshelled peanuts on the dining alcove table, wishing Jane was there instead of Mitchell. But Jane was out, at school. "We'll eat later," Mitchell had said when he saw her appear. He turned off the stove and walked closer to her and opened the bathrobe, running his hands lightly over her breast.

"Dig it," he whispered. Then he took her hand, and she let him pull her into the bedroom. He sat down on the wood-framed bed that the Italian couple before them had left behind. The bedposts were painted a gaudy gold like the cheap bureau. Lilly could not see the moon from her room, as she could now lying on the examining table. Heavy drapes had hung from bent-tin curtain poles precariously strewn across the upper window frame. Mitchell pulled her across his knees on her back. She was lying startled, face up staring into his mustache. She felt his hands on her sex and by then she was edging off him, and onto her back on the bed.

He unzipped his white sailor pants, started undoing his belt.

His fingers still seemed beautiful, like marble stones tipped with mica, but then they raked at her sides as he gently positioned himself on top of her, each of his hands clasped onto her ribs. She pushed at his chest, pushing him away. He slunk off her. She could sense Mitchell's letdown; *an attractive man like Mitchell could get any woman*, Lilly thought. Her own face was always so tense, it burned. She was volatile and inadequate. He was a small, soft-muscled man, and she would be fierce under him tonight if she let herself go.

Lilly lay still beside him under the sheets now, naked. Mitchell tried once more to caress her breasts. But when Mitchell's body pressed on her, it made her breasts feel like a toothache. "I'm sorry," she said as he stopped touching her.

"Lilly." His eyes were spacey, an emptiness in his voice. "This situation is getting very intense," he said.

She remembered how she had romanticized everything about him when, weeks ago, he first lay her on the bed and told her she was beautiful. His mustache was a tiny shrub from a thicket in another world. He was like a pure animal, his warm brawn fully possessing her. It had felt good; she didn't hesitate to lie back for him.

"Please, Lilly." Now Mitchell's chin touched a spot below her nipple, his tongue licked a dimpled circle as he lay beside her. His fingers moved to stroke the circle. She saw his beautiful hands again, but when he dropped his head on her chest, below her bosom, and leaned so heavily on her ribs—his hands going under his chin—he could have been a boy sucking at her. She felt strangely emptied and used. Mitchell touching her body only diminished Lilly, painfully.

She wished to be warm and oblivious, taken into a delirium such as a protected child feels on a winter's night, when someone very large and enveloping is responsible for her wellbeing. Responsible, too, for her life and death, and the molecules inside her that might explode from her desire to be loved so overwhelmingly. Her wish was a kind of lust, hungrier than any other she felt. She might settle for being cared for and chastised, but her body's yearnings had become primitive, insatiable.

Lilly shuttered her eyes closed, listening to sounds of the cold slum night outside after Mitchell stopped touching her and fell into sleep. The street noises below them were muffled by the half-shut window, but Lilly heard a drunken bum stranded outside the locked door of the Salvation Army shelter, wheezing and wailing.

Mitchell reached for her again after an hour. *Maybe aroused,* she had thought, *by his own dreams.* He was half-asleep, but he pulled at her hair. She knew he was trying to caress it, but his touch only threatened her again. Still, she would have let him have her that night as he tried again in his half-sleep, rolling on top of her. But even barely awake, he read her body like a traffic sign and drove off, redirected back into whatever he was dreaming and desiring before he moved to her. He rolled onto his right side, his back to her. Lilly looked away, to the window. The bum was still crying somewhere down the street, and his plaintive noise made her feel, somehow, that she wasn't all alone. Then her own fatigue overtook her, and she finally fell into a restless sleep.

Mitchell got up before Lilly the next morning. He dressed quietly, quickly, and left the apartment very early. The sun had already risen, the milkman was delivering bottles to the Salvation Army shelter across the street, cars were gunning their motors to unfreeze the long, cold night's hold on their engines.

When Lilly rose, she set her alarm clock to time her writing. She had to look for work in the neighborhood before her afternoon classes started at Sarah Lawrence College. All of a sudden, Lilly felt that she needed to urinate urgently. She pulled down her panties when she got inside the tiny bathroom, and the rounded bulb was nestled between her thighs. She thought, first, it was not a part of her, but when she put her finger to touch it, it was her own labia swelling into the shape of a large teardrop. She stood, staring at it, and the need to empty her bladder vanished.

Sitting on the toilet seat cover, still undressed, she had waited nearly an hour for her illumination to pass. And then she wasn't so much afraid as beguiled by the presence of this phantom part that seemed to carry within itself a trembling she could not control. The mysterious bulb filled her along with the salty bathroom air—the tiles and salmon-pink walls bringing her into a wild sense of being in and out of reality. It was as if she had fallen a long way down into her own immense confusion. The hole she found herself in was a sea—shadows and currents. Later she had only a fragile clarity of what the bulb had looked like that first time in the bathroom, and how it had breathed as a part of her in the beginning.

Lilly looked back on this as the morning when her world changed, the morning she finally fell apart, and her being, shifting in and out of reality, became so sensitive that it ached along with the bulb.

₪

"All right, Lillian." Beverly walked back into the examination room now. She clutched a pair of latex gloves inside a packet in her hand. "Why haven't you taken your clothes off yet? We need to get on with the examination," she said.

While Beverly opened drawers to the pearl-white cabinets by the door, tossing around some of the instruments inside them, Lilly positioned her head under the ceiling light a little better. She roused up just a tiny bit, so she could make out her own face's shape and form in a reflection the window threw. The structure of her face looked the same as when she'd checked it yesterday: she had her father's sallow complexion and dark brown hair, but unlike him, her brown eyes were almond-shaped, her nose neither small nor large for her face, but ambiguously sized, as if it weren't fully grown yet. She had her father's slender build, too. She seemed, to herself, camouflaged inside a well-proportioned but androgynous body. Nothing on her was very large, or matured, or developed.

Beverly lay the gloves inside their packet on a countertop. Then Beverly walked to the sink, turned the faucet on, and made an icing of soap bubbles, cleansing her hands, her wrists, and arms.

When she stopped squirting soap on her hands from the dispenser on the sink's rim she rinsed them in a clear stream, flapped her fingers out in the air. Drops of whitish water sprinkled the floor, the sides of the medicine bins and cabinets. She took the gloves out of their torn packet and peeled the rubber gloves onto her clean fingers.

Beverly steeled herself a little before she went to Lilly, a small blue towel in one of her gloved hands.

"What's going to happen to me?" Lilly asked her. "Can I go home?"

"Are you confused again, Lillian?" Beverly said. "You're in a psychiatric hospital. You took an overdose of Librium. You've been admitted as a voluntary patient. Dr. Burkert saw you for your initial interview, do you remember? You showed signs of extreme pelvic discomfort. He has ordered me to examine you."

"He told me no one would touch me," Lilly said. "Dr. Burkert promised me there wouldn't be any examination."

"Oh, I doubt that. Perhaps you were mishearing him." Beverly pointed three fingers to the thick leather of Lilly's belt. "Can you please take your pants down? Panties off," she said. Then, more softly, she whispered, "Try, Lillian. Lie back and take the rest of your clothes off now. You can put this towel over you. You'll feel better. No one's going to hurt you."

Between Lilly's legs, the strange inflation—the bulb—undulated. She didn't trust that it was nothing, but she started to pull at her jeans.

"Good, Lillian. Now, take them off."

Lilly undid her blue jeans' leather belt. She would never be able to describe what she felt, but it was absolute now. The bulb between her legs was not of this world, so she was crazy. All indications were that she belonged here, in this hospital, on this mental ward.

Slowly, Lilly pressed her forehead against her knees and forced herself to unbuckle her belt. She was afraid, but she rejected her tears, pulling down on her blue jeans and then lifting up her buttocks, and thrusting the jeans finally off her.

She had to cooperate now, or it could be worse for her, she thought. She grabbed at the thin towel Beverly was dangling, and it scraped across her naked knees as she tried to cover her exposed thighs. Then she saw Beverly had turned her back on her. The room was suddenly colder—with its awful sterile tools and medical implements—so when Lilly pulled down her white cotton panties at last, shivering, the air that hit her was like a wind kicking at her skin.

She lay back down on her back, letting her panties drop off the edge of the examination table to the ceramic tiled floor. She lay flat on her back on the metal table and closed her eyes.

The loud shuffling of the nurse frightened her. There were harsh sounds, more drawers opening and shutting. Lilly didn't understand why the room was darkening until she opened her eyes again and saw Beverly had pulled down the metal shutters of the window. The moonlight and city lights had vanished behind them.

It seemed like seconds passed before Beverly spun around again, to her. "Well, are we ready now?" Beverly glanced at the puddle of Lilly's clothes on the floor. "Okay, I guess we are, then," she said. "Does anything hurt?" Beverly was asking Lilly now. Beverly's gloved hand pushed down on Lilly's abdomen. "We're exploring externally first," she explained.

From Lilly's thigh to her navel, the nurse's right hand repeated its mechanical actions, pressed and released with its heel. "Does this hurt?" Beverly kept asking each time her hand bounced off a spot. "How about here? Do you feel pain anywhere in the back area?"

The room's light now came from an overhead swing lamp that Lilly hadn't seen Beverly flick on, its beam lancing Lilly's groin.

The room was lit, but strange and dark and coffinlike, as in a movie theater.

"When you were admitted there were notes about your discomfort," Beverly was saying. "Dr. Burkert just wanted to be sure. Of course, if your pain is hysterical you must use the hospital to explore the reasons why."

The motion of Beverly's hands stopped, and for a long minute she stared straight into Lilly's eyes.

Suddenly, Lilly couldn't bear this cold woman in her perfection. Beverly's voice came to her now in half-sounds. The mysterious bulb inside Lilly rose, swelling—the same apparition she had seen that day in the bathroom in her Little Italy apartment, suffocating her in its waves of distress and unwanted heat. Lilly felt herself on the verge of fire.

"Do you know why Dr. Burkert wanted this exam?" Beverly was saying, still talking at her. Lilly couldn't answer, and Beverly shuffled to the cabinets and counter once again. She started checking the different probing utensils: black electric instruments connected to one long holder fastened to the white wall, the plugs of their coiling black cords pressed into one central outlet. Each of the three instruments resembled a telephone receiver; switched on, Lilly felt them as flashlights.

"I'm going to ask you to slide down more." Beverly gestured with her right forefinger, signaling Lilly to position herself as she came back to the table, flexing her fingers in the gloves.

When Lilly slid her back against the table, she heard the paper tear and she struggled to sit up, but the nurse abruptly grabbed a hold of Lilly's feet, clasped her ankles, and tugged at her. Pulling out the stirrups, she forced Lilly's feet into them, leaving a wide spread between Lilly's thighs and her naked genitals.

Lilly weakly fought to sit up again, but her feet were imprisoned in the stirrups. "I'm not going to argue with you," Beverly said. "I don't argue with patients. I'm staff, you know." Beverly's hand was doing what it did before, pressing first on Lilly's lower abdomen. Beverly had flicked one of the black instruments on, and a red light beeped from its nozzle. "I'm not trying to hurt you, Lillian," she said.

The fingers were somewhere, and Lilly helplessly lay her hands, palms up, along her sides. She stiffened, tightening against an unbearable onrushing, a heated current inside her.

There was another silence before Beverly, taking no notice of the reflexive reactions erupting now in the body she was probing, said, "I have to finish this. Please stop squirming, for heaven's sake."

When the darkness came, cloaking and then wrapping Lilly into mute stillness, the tips of Beverly's rubber-gloved fingers were cold, like buds of ice. But Lilly's mind was already crashing behind her. If she could not die she could become a person who had fallen into a certain kind of death, she thought.

She started driving there with her jerks and swallows. Her physical body was hurling torn shreds and pieces of the examination table paper in a tantrum, and she was screaming. But then—she was past her body, as if a space had blown out, taking everything with it into a great expansive nothing, an in-rushing of gas and matter and darkness.

She felt the gloved fingers of the nurse. They were warm now, and brought her into a feeling that some better power was over her, unfolding Lilly into a safe night of protectors and caretakers. Fracture and genesis were happening both at once inside her. First, falling in pieces, she was now coming back into the reality of the room, of her mental breakdown. And then, within seconds, she could feel her body again, as if after a long disemboweling.

Lilly looked up into the eyes of the nurse. Beverly was no longer Lilly's tormentor. The nurse would help her, Lilly thought, and Lilly would not have to go back, into the outside world. Not for a long while.

﬘

Two hours later, Lilly awoke from a cloudy sleep inside a seclusion room, conscious of her surroundings again. When Lilly had stopped screaming, Beverly had helped her stand. Two aides had rushed in the examination room, held Lilly by each elbow, and escorted her down the hall—dressed only with a sheet around her shoulders, into this barren white room down the hall. They had helped her dress into a thick gown, told her she was in the "quiet room." Then they forced her to drink down a watery liquid with crushed pieces of sedating pills in it.

Now Lilly was listening to herself breathing too hard. Underneath her back was the cold plastic of the bare mattress. Around her and above—a pure whiteness with no shadows. The room's severe and thickly padded walls were painted with a heavy, chalky coat like milk of magnesia, their stuffing worming a way out through holes.

She had come through the examination, but she was mad. *It could be something beautiful*, she thought, her madness. She would make it have sense, like the strange symbols she once saw in the basement of her parents' house, where her mother's ancient Hebraic texts lay.

Lilly fell back to the thoughts of the alchemy she had researched in the Sarah Lawrence library. In the quiet now, she tried to remember the alchemy pictures she saw in the books. There was a place for what was happening to her within those images, she thought. All this wouldn't feel so strange if she could remember what she read in the books at the Sarah Lawrence library.

"She appears calm," Lilly suddenly heard now.

Two people walked into the room.

Lilly struggled to sit up on the mattress.

"You gave us a pretty hard time, Lillian." It was Beverly talking down to her. "The way you were screaming—"

"Wait, Beverly—," the man said to the nurse. He was lean, not tall. "I'm Dr. Burkert," he said. "I admitted you after the emergency room. Do you remember? We thought it better to protect you in here while you were having such a difficult time."

Lilly fell back into a sound of plastic, but she felt relief, hearing his voice.

"We're going to talk in here," she heard him say to the nurse. And when Lilly again looked up there was only Dr. Burkert in the room: slender-boned and young, he was almost sympathetic-looking in his chino trousers, his moss desert boots. His long hair was caramel-colored, and it curtained his ears. "I'm concerned," he said to Lilly, "about what happened to you a few hours ago. Can you tell me what happened?"

"I was committed," she said.

"You weren't committed. You signed a voluntary admission form in the emergency room. Perhaps it's hard for you to remember everything that has happened. We'll take our time, all right?" Lilly recognized his clipped-sounding accent now. It was South African. He talked like the man on that *Safari to Africa* TV series on Channel 13. She hadn't noticed he really wasn't British when he interviewed her before. She had been sure he was British. "Do you understand why you were admitted to the hospital?" he asked her again now.

"Someone brought me here."

"A woman named Jane brought you to the emergency room tonight. Your roommate at college, I believe."

Lilly felt a slight throb in her bare right foot, like warm blood was suddenly flowing down her instep. Someone had forgotten to put her socks and Frye boots back on.

She heard his breathing in what she believed was his exasperation at her. "You mentioned a feeling of discomfort inside your body. I ordered a pelvic examination," he said.

Lilly clasped her hands around both her arms, keeping her body lying flat and stretched on her back.

The fresh cotton of her underwear felt suddenly too warm against the inside of her nervous thighs, against her buttocks. The dark gulf inside her was a basin of tears, anger, and helplessness.

Lilly firmed her eyes shut. It could be that the doctor knew nothing about her at all. And it was best to keep it that way.

"You were very frightened in the examination room," he said. "And then you were out of control. We gave you some Valium to take some of the panic away."

She lay as stiffly as she could and looked up at the ceiling to keep herself still. Her eyes searched the white ceiling, the lightbulbs behind the translucent square plastic tiles. She wondered if any flies were caught between the plastic and the masked light fixtures the way they were in her parents' house in Bedford on summer nights. Moths died, scorched into dust by flying into the lights.

"All right, then," he said. "We'll give you more time to calm down."

Lilly waited but she didn't hear Dr. Burkert's voice again, and she didn't move or speak in the new silence.

She felt more than heard Dr. Burkert stepping back. His soft-soled shoes made a squeak on the floor, and he said, as if even a sound might have frightened her, "I think you'll find the hospital to be a safe place."

The door closed, and the door lock caught behind him as he left.

₪

Lilly sat up on the mattress again, after Dr. Burkert left the quiet room. *Would he come back?* She wondered, and then she was thinking of Mitchell in Little Italy, of lying on the synthetic gold brocade spread waiting for Mitchell to come into her bedroom the way it was, before her feelings changed.

Mitchell liked to find Lilly with only her wild baby-blue high heels on, naked as these walls, she remembered. She would listen as Mitchell pulled a beer out of the refrigerator in the kitchen. "Now you look like a woman," Mitchell would say, walking into the bedroom to lie with her.

Now Lilly forced herself off the mattress. She was like a child, tortured by her own violent motions. She scraped toward the locked door. Her hand stroked its flaky white surface. It wasn't wood, she was sure, but a strange cement or plaster.

She could break out. Soon the doctor would be gone for the night, and if she waited a clearing would be apparent to her outside in the hall. She pushed her right forefinger inside the keyhole, filled, too, with dusty white crust. The whole room was overpainted with that terrible white, so thickly layered the space was unnatural and frightening.

No, she did not want to break out, she thought. She took her finger out of the keyhole, and then she put it into her mouth, as if to taste her own incarceration, make love to it. She wanted to stay. In the hospital, she would be safe. The doctor was right.

Through the door's synthetic plastic window, the people milling around the ward were blurred and murky. A middle-aged woman trying to pull her hospital dress down because it kept sliding up her doughy legs. Two adolescent girls passing a bag of Frito-Lay corn chips back and forth from one another's hands as they sat cross-legged on the hall carpet. Someone complaining to a chubby nurse. Then a teenage girl started yelling and screaming. The girl broke from two aides trying to calm her and ran away, down the corridor.

Lilly stepped back from the door. She raised her right, throbbing bare foot. She thought she felt a flow of blood dripping from its heel. But when she bent to touch the liquid, there was no blood, and her foot felt cold. It was as if all the heat in her had been spent. The small bloodless footprints she made stepping back from the door could have been a ghost's.

A soft haze sailed over Lilly's thoughts.

Chapter Two

Lilly was seventeen years old the summer of her father's accident. She was still living in the house with her parents.

Two strokes. One caused David, her father, to tumble down the stairs. David's second stroke made him fall on the kitchen floor. But Lilly was upstairs, with her bathroom door shut by then. Her mother, Helen, was out for the afternoon at that time, at a friend's house down the road.

"Take this bag of your father's things, Lilly," Helen had said in David's hospital room, pushing at Lilly, later that night, after the ambulance came and took them to the hospital. David's slight body was tucked tightly inside the white bedsheets of the bed in the intensive care unit at Northern Westchester Hospital. "The men in the ambulance took his watch," her mother had said to her, and Lilly remembered how David lay unconscious on the kitchen floor after his second stroke—her mother frantically dialing the emergency number on the refrigerator door.

The sight of David immersed inside the coma, lying cocooned and breathing through his nose like a wound, made Lilly paralyzed. Her father had turned to ether, she had thought. She could feel him turned inside-out and vaporous and faraway.

Her mother was wagging the plastic bag at her. "Maybe these ambulance people were stealing. I have his wallet. But there was not his watch to be found anywhere. I don't want this bag, Lillian, I don't want it anymore." Helen had held up a plastic bag, and Lilly saw her father's box of peppermint Chiclets in it, his gold pinkie ring with its tiny blue stone, which she never knew the name of, and other things—all floating inside the sterilized plastic bag like tiny fish: loose change, his click dispenser of "sen-sen" breath fresheners . . . "The nurses gave me this bag," Helen was saying. "What am I supposed to do with the bag? Everything this man ruins." Helen's foreign accent had entered the hollow of David's hospital room. Her mother's eyes were vacant and swollen, and Lilly heard the way Helen speaks when Helen needed her own language again, the Hebrew inflections returned to Helen's speech. "What am I expected to do now? What do you want from me? You are so selfish you do not hear when your father falls." She had stopped, but only to collect more thrust. "Shame on you," she said. "Shame on you and your father."

Her mother was a force too disintegrating to be near. Helen was more an atmosphere in the room than a person. She talked right through Lilly.

Under them, in his bed, her father's face had twitched in his coma; his lips were making a hissing noise through his teeth.

"I want to go back home and get some sleep, " Helen had finally said. "Your father isn't the only one who must have rest. What did he do, Lilly? What is all this?"

Helen had brushed her hand through Lilly's hair and taken a Kleenex out of her purse to wipe Lilly's face. "What is the matter with you now, darling?" she asked Lilly. "Look at you, you're a mess."

Helen spit into a Kleenex, running the tissue over Lilly's cheeks with its moistened end, and Lilly had felt a relief for an instant. Helen's hand was in her hair, and she was against her mother's chest and Helen was holding her. Helen drew Lilly to the linen of her summer shift and the feel of her mother's body underneath it that was soft.

₪

How many times had Lilly gone over every detail of that night? *This is how it had happened*, Lilly told herself in the seclusion room again now. Helen was leaving in two days, an early morning flight for Tel Aviv. Her parents were separating. Her mother was going to return to Israel to spend some time. The memory of that night—David's accident, his room in intensive care lingered now in the whiteness of the seclusion room. The fragments of what had happened in the house would not reassemble inside Lilly's head with any clarity, darkening and drifting away from her as they had for three years since it happened—mental clouds harboring an accumulation of storm.

She remembered the draft in the bathroom from the open window that night, the smell of pussy willows and birch trees when she had undressed to take her evening bath. The bathroom was so old, the pipes had grated and squeaked like metal grinders when the hot water ran. For a summer night, the weather had been cool. Lilly had turned off the faucet for her bath, and the water was so clear and clean. Disrobing, Lilly had gotten into the water when she heard the dull thud below her, as if a piece of furniture had fallen down. It was an old, nineteenth-century colonial house, and the floorboards were fragile and did not muffle sounds. But then something within Lilly took over, the bathwater was already riding up into her in caressing waves, circulating sexual pleasures. The sound of the impact had vanished from her awareness, and Lilly slipped into the warm seduction of the water as if she were in the middle of a dream. She pushed herself down into the warmth, and the bathwater had felt like a blanketing body holding her close to her mother, not letting her go. She had stayed in the water longer than she usually did, enveloped by it. Then she heard her mother's car in the driveway, and seconds later—Helen's loud footsteps, the front door downstairs opening. Her mother was home again.

"What happened?" Helen was screaming to Lilly from the stairway. "What happened here, you tell me!" and then Lilly was in a half-blind whirlwind of regrets. Lilly leaped out of the bath and put on her robe as Helen's shrieks split the silence.

Later, Lilly thought she had no memories of the night her father fell into his coma on the kitchen floor, except those planted and fixed into her body from her mother's furious sobs. She could only partly remember those moments she had heard the thud sound of her father's second fall. It was if a liquid amnesia flowed down and through her every time she tried to recall her hesitation that night, submerging her again in oblivion.

₪

Down in the basement of her parents' house in Bedford, next to her mother's book-binding craft tools which lay on a workbench, Lilly once furtively found an old photograph of her parents' wedding in New York that Helen accidentally forgot to put back into her private, locked chest one afternoon. The newspaper clipping from a *White Plains Reporter Dispatch* of 1946 read, "DRINK A TANGERINE! A BRIGHT NEW TASTE THAT'S REALLY DIFFERENT!" and "AUNT PRISCILLA WAS SO PRISSY SHE WORE HERSELF OUT STARCHING CLOTHES—" and in the middle was the announcement of the marriage between her exotic, foreign mother, Helen, to her American father, David, at the Hotel Astor in New York City.

There were dark curtains with birds and sailboats on them in the photos and long white gloves over her mother's muscular, freckled arms. Helen Gilderstein became Helen Weill dressed in suede Joan Crawford platform shoes, and a white sunbonnet with pearls on its rim, her strong fingers in the pictures of the wedding dipping into expensive chocolate mousses and into shining glasses of champagne. . . .

A British education at the University of London laced her mother's manners. Helen never talked about old Jerusalem where she was born and spent her childhood—the daughter of a wealthy, aristocratic Jewish businessman in British-occupied Palestine—except when she struggled to pronounce American words. In other photos, Lilly saw the younger, voluptuous Helen, in a cotton dress with white lace neckline and sandals, smiling widely inside a limestone arch against shadows of barren and cratered hills.

Inside the living room of the American house in Westchester when Lilly was young, Helen had put a painting of Old Jerusalem up over the colonial fireplace: Jagged brushstrokes of women walking . . . the white-green olive trees had heads like pulled cotton. A smoky, strange painting with no footing, nothing firm. People, houses, and trees like clouds. Faint impressions were left on Lilly's memory from when Helen took her to Jerusalem as a very young child of two and, again, when Lilly was eight years old: yellowed photo stills of dead and lost cousins, shadows lost in vistas of sun-whitened earth and beautiful four-winged houses built at the time of the British Mandate, before the state of Israel was declared, and almost all the streets named for poets and sages who had lived in Spain in the Golden Age.

Old photos showed an underground cistern where Helen and her older sister, Edna, bathed as children, catching the precious rainwater for cooking and their baths some time in 1920s. The terraces were filled with calla lilies and the leathery leaves of pomegranate trees potted in giant ceramic vases. There were garden tearooms in other photos, British Tommies with khaki shorts, and military batons with leather handles strapped to their wrists, patrolling the streets and neighborhoods. In later family albums, there were photos of rows of women in army shorts and brown boots weaving the blue-and-white national flag of *Eretz Yisrael*, the Star of David that hung over the limestone porches of the Jewish population by the 1940s . . . scraps of information and glimpses that Lilly could piece together into a story of Helen's past.

There were many scenes of the vanquished places and its cities behind the Ancient Walls in the albums—snatches, shuffled and reshuffled through Helen's fingers, mystical-like pieces gathered up in old photo stills.

A woman's pubis was a bulb, Lilly once thought, remembering the first time, as a child, she saw her mother's naked body. Helen had left the door open to her bedroom, which her mother would then do frequently. Helen had undressed in full oblivion; Lilly was in the hall and she could see her mother's wide-open body. The view was brief and blazing, telling Lilly that every part of Helen was grand, that she occupied all space, there was no one else there, there were no other bodies in the room, not even David, the place he had in the bedsheets covered by her mother's messy underthings—Helen was the only one, and it was beyond seduction. Her mother had stopped what she was doing, intoxicated with herself, not even aware of Lilly coming upon her. Her mother's nakedness, curves of soft flesh, was like an enormous fruit, Lilly had thought, encountering, as she stared through the huge gap in the door, the intimate details of Helen's body, her mother's sex—a fine apricot-colored down, a pit at its center. The large woman was giving Lilly exhilarating access to Lilly's own being, like a mirror that blinds. Helen's two round, moist eyes were a source of liquid starlight that none of her mother's frequent mood swings or fits of temper could ever take away for good. Helen was a pure energy and spread out before Lilly in an abandon without shame until the air drove Lilly to the edge of an abyss. Even the memory of it made Lilly feel again like she was becoming nothing, and that the tension inside her own body was the need to remain mute and stilled, as she stared into the masturbatory excitement of the figure who seemed to absorb all the spaces of the earth.

Helen had her own stories of Palestine before the wars and of the exotic cities of Cairo and Beirut, the old countries of Persia and Egyptian Babylon. Helen's past had vanished, but where had it gone? Lilly had asked herself as a child. Helen loved showing Lilly the pictures of her childhood in Palestine. "Outside the house on Palmach there was a basin where Edna was in charge of bathing me," Helen told Lilly. "You see my sister Edna with her long braids? All the time, she took great pride in cutting my hair and touching me like I am nothing but hers and only a doll!"

Helen had studied to be a nurse at the Hadassah Hospital to get out of the *Haganah*, and then Helen went in the opposite direction to the refugee ships coming to the port of Haifa, to New York where she married soon, as if on an impulse. Helen was only twenty-one when she met David, a law student at Columbia University.

Helen never explained why she stopped going back to her old house in Jerusalem, taking Lilly with her, but only that she could no longer recognize the places of her youth there anymore by 1960. And now—Helen had no home, except with Lilly here, in the Bedford house.

But Helen knew of a world more enchanted than any other, and downstairs, in the basement of the house in Westchester, a certified hand bookbinder, she practiced her bookbinding craft, creating her world again from old texts and etchings, perpetuating the tales as though they were spells she could cast upon herself.

Ancient Hebrew and Aramaic texts full of alchemical symbols and cabalistic etchings arrived by special parcel post to the house in Bedford where Lilly lived with her parents before she left for college. Helen was commissioned by museums in Jerusalem to re-sew and repair the texts using buckram or full leather fine-bindings. The certificate from London University with Helen's maiden name, "Gilderstein," printed in English in bold black letters spelling out "Master Bookbinder," too, hung in a frame above her mother's worktable. "And no such certificate exists in the United States," Helen once told Lilly.

The seasonal winds of Bedford flowed under the rusty hinges of the basement door where Helen's bookbinding work tools lay. As a young girl, Lilly could feel the boiler heating the basement room along with the gentle quiet when Helen hung her old leathers up, clothed in the dust of the biblical lands. *The texts had souls*, Lilly once thought.

Lilly could see the specially treated papers and leathers hung dripping by clothespins on a string above the worktable. In the photos of Helen in Westchester, she looked heavy and too tough, overshadowed by the perfect lawns and delicate surroundings. Her body simply did not translate here in America, nor into Westchester fashions: the A-line shifts, the boxy suits and jackets, and the Capri pants all conspired to make her look like a misfit in a landscape of white colonial houses and Chevrolet Impalas. Helen grew increasingly nervous with her American neighbors and acquaintances; she stumbled through words, laughed too loud, her face taking on the tension lines of a woman who was terrified of ridicule and pity. The two sets of albums were so radically different. Her mother leaning against the Jerusalem limestone arches and pillars, full and smiling and dangerous in the first albums, but everything was dangerous in Helen's native country, and Helen, wearing her elegant cardigans and European-style plain cotton dress with necklines of lace, had looked like the most civilized, sophisticated object in the picture. She could have been an imported confection, her smile sweet as a flower in the sun.

The house in Bedford was still as Helen worked and, seating her on the basement floor, the damp seeped into Lilly's legs. Lilly could feel the calm near her mother's bookbinding tools and the workbench.

The sun went down and Lilly stayed with Helen in her smock, inside her puffy comforts. Helen brought down cocoa for them to drink, plates of graham crackers and Hopjes candies.

Lilly studied Helen. A full woman whose short but strong fingers produced a special wizardry, which was unseen, unheard by others. Here, her mother shuffled back and forth on the basement floor from the hanging leathers to the soiled and tattered editions of the old Hebrew texts—the reddish, unkempt hair under Helen's headscarf like the soft threads she used on the bindings of the resurrected books. Her mother had a tempestuous soul. Lilly saw her as a mistress of dislocation, a temporary insanity, filling Lilly with intoxicating ideas about ancient powers and reawakened spirits.

The bookbinding workplace was filled with bewitching lusts, as if it were a bedroom for lovers. Helen beat the hides of the beautiful olive and brown leathers. The room was pungent with the smells of the shredded leather shavings and the old book pages—holey and aged like soft, moldy cheeses. The sweet pastes hardened, and the wind underneath the basement door blew the delicate shavings and dusts to scatter, her mother's fingers stained with dyes and glue. Helen's smock was splashed with mending potions that were viscous and liquid and spread a magic through the ends of the torn pages, so that Lilly could see the outskirts of vanished ancient cities again and deep silences that still lay in the country Helen had lost with pictures of Abraham and God.

Helen strained her hands to get the dimensions and measurements precise, moving swiftly from a table of rulers and measuring tapes to the tables where the old books lay, waiting for her to bring them out of their long sleep. Helen's face heated and flushed, beaming enchantment. The basement floor splattered with the elements that brought the books back into life: gold dust, shavings, the cutting tools that made designs on the beautiful backings and spines, the inlays and inscriptions Helen restored. Helen applied different silvers and golds, which she melted in a pot over a Bunsen burner to turn into liquid before applying to the newly engraved letterings.

"I love you, I love you," Helen used to say to Lilly when Lilly was small, and they were alone in the big house after grade school. "My darling, my darling—," Helen said, imitating Zsa Zsa Gabor, as Lilly lay swept in her mother's arms. Lilly's shirt and skirt were almost torn by her mother's embrace.

"Mom, you're crazy."

"I know." Helen's voice was impassioned. The smell of orange marmalade was on her breath, and Helen's big hefty arms were cotton and stone all at once.

Many times there were no reasons for her mother's rages. No before or after. Helen shook Lilly hard in her arms; she wouldn't let Lilly go. Helen's terry-cloth robe opened at the breasts that loomed out like two animals. Her mother set Lilly up on her two feet suddenly; she pulled Lilly's head squarely in front of her own bristling red face, enlarging in every crease.

When Helen's rage erupted, the floor itself was rocking, unstable. She squatted on the floor and put Lilly over her knee, spanking her with an open hand. Helen's knee knifed through to Lilly's groin, and Lilly felt her nightshirt ripping as if it were her own skin. A volcano might have been surging from under the colonial wood boards, hot and deadly, purging Lilly, casting her, split, onto an unknown shore.

The Westchester moon and other faraway planets floated like distant buoys inside the confusion of Lilly's dreams. The wind seemed to carry a fire up through the veiny blue clouds, and sometimes Lilly dreamed that her house in Bedford was lost inside distant craters and burning up. She imagined the secret parts of her own body and its vulva as a planet, a glowing bulb far above the stonescape of the land, exploding into lava. She read once in an old schoolbook about Ferdinand Magellan, and how he discovered the planet Venus through his telescope in the night, and how Venus was covered with opaque clouds made of sulfuric acids, which showed him evidence of "extreme volcanism," though it was an enigma, the book explained, and Lilly could not understand it either. All she knew then could turn into Magellanic Clouds like the ones she read about in her schoolbooks, small galaxies, white and nebulous, held in the grip of the ruthless Milky Way.

It was where the dead and forgotten and obscure vanished, people like the people of her mother's country, Palestine. Lilly thought she could see them sometimes in the spaces between dream and wakefulness. History fascinated her; she thought lost beings, who might never be found again, were lost somewhere in the Magellanic Clouds. She tried to imagine what the Magellanic Clouds had looked like from her bedroom window but remembered instead Helen's hands in the basement, over her bookbinding tools in the afternoon when everything around felt as drowsy as she.

₪

Lying flat on the mattress now in the seclusion room, Lilly managed to settle herself back into some place of relief between exhaustion and sleep as some of the luscious allegories in Helen's bookbinding texts filled her mind. She saw the figure of Maria, the alchemist, floating before her eyes, with her spectacular smile, and it felt as if rain had started pricking Lilly, from a sky that noticed her suffering in fire, watering tender shoots to perforate a space between destruction and becoming. As in an execution, when the condemned prisoner experiences an ecstasy an instant before death, or like a lover at climax, Lilly leaped to escape that moment before a final disintegration. But she didn't know what to call what she was experiencing, and it horrified her, stalked her. She would have to look it up in her books.

She felt a sharp hunger in her stomach, an emptiness now. Her tears were beginning again. The night of her father's accident was returning to her in flickers. She saw the bathroom in the Bedford house, the bathwater. In her parents' bedroom, suitcases had lain half-packed for days already, hatboxes filled with Helen's toiletries, her collections of scattered paraphernalia from twenty years in America. The truth of that night both choked and eluded Lilly again. *Guilty*, Lilly thought now, she was *guilty*. If her father were injured her mother would have to stay. A dumbfounded culpability took hold of her again.

She touched her hand with a finger from the other, as if holding two realities in each and trying now to connect them, like circuits or tangled fire hazards without protection. Her hand had become thin enough to see the blue branches of her nervous system. It wasn't that she fractured, she thought, but that the enmeshed wires inflamed her, turned her whole heart into fire. Her mind went back to the examination room, the hefty nurse touching her, and the convulsion that threw her back until she was light and pure again. She fell into pieces to stop the fire, she thought, and now she needed to reconnect all the circuits inside her.

Lilly rubbed her neck. She smoothed out the hurt muscles, searched for bruises with alert eyes. The tantrum in the examination room ripped some skin on her arms. She wondered if the skin tears were from the stronghold of the nurse; a bruise was on her right arm. She saw it, wincing. She touched it, and the pain brought a kind a sweetness to her agony, a war wound, she told herself, a wound suffered only because she had fought for her life. It was a kind of animal inside her, the absolute take-over of impulses in her body she could not control. If existence meant she would be a splat on the floor, she didn't want to exist, she thought now. The pains and aches subsided as she stared around the padded white walls.

She didn't know how long they would keep her here, but she was slowly being allowed her own feelings again. It was not so much a prison cell to her, though the door was firmly shut, but the room began to take on the feeling of a cool white space, and she moaned without fear, as if she had wanted this incarceration for a long time, this escape from her terror of conflagration. All she required was that she be left light and pure and not in flames. Even the memory of the nurse Beverly was slowly becoming as impersonal as the white walls, and now she could feel her own body again. Even the pain and the bruises helped her feel her own body again, took it out of the numbness into which she had escaped the real world and its unbearable threats of incendiary intimacies.

Lilly went back to the mattress and sat again on its plastic. She let herself feel the harsh isolation of the white room. Her breathing was slowly measuring the beats of her freedom from the real world now, she thought. She stared up at the peels and flakes of white on the ceiling.

Was there a thread somewhere that would start to reveal a whole fierce and subtle weave inside her? She slowly allowed herself to lie back on the pillowless mattress. But drifting into a light half-sleep, Lilly felt alienated from her body again as she lay still on the mattress. Soon she heard in a dream the cold nurse telling her to undress. She felt the cold nurse's condescension, saw her wet eyes. The nurse was pulling on her latex gloves to handle her in the half-conscious dream, and a tangled ball of confusions was tossing around in Lilly's head, sensations returning like ghosts swarming up her spine, swelling with the sweet sting of excitement trying to envelop her. Forced by her sudden terror, she jolted into a full wakefulness. She jumped off the mattress.

Lilly felt her skin flushing. She scrambled in her mind for some logical progression of events and causes she could write down or figure out, but it was elusive, frightening, unobtainable. She felt the bulb again as if it were a bird between her legs, fluttering, trying to take flight. When it was not throbbing inside her it was still within her body, she thought, sleeping and waiting. She had looked up the word "bulb" in the giant, unabridged Webster's dictionary inside the library at Sarah Lawrence.

"Bulb: An underground shoot in the soil, keeping the storage of food for the yet unborn plant for when it can bloom."

Suddenly, a noise outside the quiet room door startled her, and she listened hard on the mattress, but this time she was afraid it was the doctor again. He would be back any minute asking her more questions about her father, the accident, Helen, the bulb, everything. Surfaces could be perishable in his hands, she told herself, and she felt an emptiness gnaw at her, not chaos or turbulence but an abysmal, indissoluble, exasperating nothing. The bulb was shrinking away. *They would call Helen, wouldn't they?* She thought, suddenly afraid. She imagined the quiet room door opening and there, in the crack, Helen would stand in the effacing light, not the nurse Beverly nor Dr. Burkert. Lilly had been exposed now, *the bulb had been exposed*, she thought. She wasn't well, she was aberrant. She felt the burning in her back and calves again where she had hit against the metal examination table in her wild tantrum. She pulled at the icy plastic covering of the bare mattress; she felt cold here, too, in this white, unheated room. But she would not go and call for help, for a blanket. No, she would not ask them for anything. She must not ask for a thing, she told herself. It was kind of animal inside her, the absolute takeover of impulses in her body she could not control. If existence meant she would be a splat on the floor, she didn't want to exist. What had happened in the examination? Had she wet the paper in her explosion? All she remembered was the massive malfunction from within her—as if a force were moving through her flesh, her muscles went out of control—and then she had felt without a physical body at all.

Lilly watched the shadow of her thinned body on the walls. The bulb was pulsing. Nothing made any sense. She wanted to think about her father and his accident now, lying still, and waiting for what more could happen to her. But the bulb was swelling again, and it was her mother who was forcing herself into Lilly's mind, moving from remembered scene to scene.

She needed to lie still, be patient, unafraid now. Because, despite her terror, pieces of memory, fractures of time and feeling were struggling to come into focus, as if for the first time and she was safe. The vacuum inside her was stirring, an underground of groping questions swarming, moving, converging, all together, all as one, circle concentrating circle, point enveloping point, rising for a nebulous process to take shape in her—an alchemy from the impulses these three years had shackled and repressed inside her—desires and yearnings she had been harboring unaware. Substance to fill her emptiness. It was in this incarceration that she might find solutions, some relief.

Shadows were coming into her mind now, and then she was making a map for a journey backward into some realm other than her immediate life, and it included the realm of her own barely conscious memory, of the conscious secrecy of things.

Lilly scanned the pure white, soundless crucible that contained her now, the padded walls and locked door. Then she was struggling to put the last weeks of her life back into some order and clarity, before tonight's moments of madness, her final fall.

Chapter Three

The walls of the apartment Lilly had shared with Jane in Little Italy were painted thickly in salmon-pink so unlike this room, with ornate moldings and golden brass doorknobs. And when Lilly lay in bed trying to write in her Little Italy apartment, there had been a glass chandelier over her head that mirrored reflections from its machine-carved, dangling icicles.

Outside the apartment there were the Albanese Fancy Meat and Poultry Store, Moe's Meat Market, and the rows of bright orange-red tenement houses, the shine of their gunmetal gates and doors. Xylophone music traveled on the clam-scented winds from Grand Street where the restaurants stood, and the gusts also carried the odors of baking bread. The steam-baked bread scents, sauces, spices, and dirt collecting into waves . . . how much the earthy streets of Little Italy had aroused her! Sometimes it made her feel herself, lose herself—admit to being a living material, too.

Two days after she discovered the bulb that first morning, she listened to herself explain to Mitchell the reasons she couldn't be with him anymore—telling him everything but that she had felt like an object to him, and now a strange bulb had appeared between her thighs, and she realized she couldn't love him at all.

The city winter snows left the apartment feeling like a damp cave. The apartment reeked with moldy floor tiles, old painted walls. The winter stopped all the movement on the streets that were thick with ice because the New York City plows came last to the poorer neighborhoods. Sarah Lawrence shut down for "bad weather."

Lilly stayed in the apartment, missing her classes at the college, and Jane returned from Sarah Lawrence in the evenings. One night, Jane bought them sandwiches that Moe made in his delicatessen—thick salami in rye bread, and sardines with tomato sauce laden with Italian olive oil. Jane and Lilly had sat together out on the balcony, on the rod-iron divan Helen gave them from the abandoned patio in Bedford—Jane with her knees brought up to her chin, eating unshelled peanuts from a bag, her lanky body wrapped in a blanket. Tall and reed-slender, Jane had yellow-white hair, soft down on her arms that bristled when she blushed which, shy, Jane did often. The neighborhood boys adored gazing up at Jane from the street whenever she ventured out on the balcony. Jane had blinked down at them, as if she were temporarily out of breath. Lilly would have imagined—with the effect made by the oily slums and dingy shops below them, their glass windows showing strings of hanging chicken heads, ham hocks, and meat carcasses inside—that Jane's face would reflect back the sordidness of their lives there. But, beyond her form, a vista surfaced of night sky and earthy, dazzling tenements and shop fronts, and Lilly did not miss Mitchell. She was no longer hurt that Mitchell hadn't tried to get her back. "Out to lunch," Jane had said, meaning to describe both her perpetually vague but dizzy mental states and the neighborhood that loomed over her shoulders.

As weeks went on, the bulb reappeared and disappeared unpredictably, without Lilly's control. It appeared at the times that the apartment was empty but something would be left of the night before with Jane—Jane's handkerchief, a bowl with unshelled peanuts or ice cream they had shared, still sitting on the kitchen table, the faint echo of a conversation they'd had in the night—a feeling that Jane was possessing her with her warmth.

Lilly started setting the alarm early, to avoid meeting Jane in the kitchen or at the divan. She was already skipping classes at Sarah Lawrence before the snows came. Slowly, Lilly was becoming familiar with crises in unreality, in which the bulb inexplicably reappeared to her. She suffered exhaustion and depletion in late January and February, as if from months and miles of pointless, directionless travel, and hours spent analyzing and thinking.

The old St. Patrick's Church stood in its dishevelment on Mulberry Street, gusts of wind driving papers and city trash into the wire fencing that hemmed in the graveyard like a chicken coop, enclosing old graves that were plasterlike, fragmentized. And Lilly had felt that if she followed the path toward the far end of the graveyard, soon she would hear the sounds of angels or unnatural fire, and the wind would blow to shreds all the boundaries between the dead and the living.

The St. Patrick's School for Boys occupied the width of an entire city block, taking up all the space between Mott and Mulberry streets. Above the doors of the Byzantine church building was a plaque that read "Divine Liturgy." The figure of the archangel Michael was a sculpture made from bronze in the run-down front entrance. But Lilly was drawn into the baptistery from the back entrance, on Mulberry Street. She followed a long, dark walkway, and there was a wire fence that hemmed the walkway from the cemetery. The vines growing around the fence and on the gravestones were so desiccated that they looked like scorpions in a cold desert.

Lilly walked through a quiet dark, following the path of the laid flagstones. She came to a sunlit cloister and stole inside the baptistery, through a tiny vestibule. She entered, pulling open a splintered, beat-up old door and sat down in a pew. She imagined the stories of boys' baptisms, boys faint from fasting, shivering in the cold, until the moment of their rite of passage. The old baptistery was rank with a Manhattan smell but still like a sanctum towering up high, an arborlike pavilion of green, gold, purple, and white mosaic from a marble floor to a domed ceiling. In the highest point of the ballooning dome was a naked Jesus standing up to his waist in a long river as an unkempt apostle poured water on him and God's disembodied hand pointed to the Holy Spirit at Jesus' head in the form of a white bird. The deteriorated stone floor had the romanticism of a forbidden dream, and Lilly had remembered kneeling before an alabaster statue of Mother Mary, inside a raw stone Lazarist monastery in Jerusalem with her mother. It was on a road called Mamilla, which the Christian Arabs called the Waters of God, and the neighborhood, off-limits to Jews, had terrible alarming military signs, threats, and warnings. "This Mother Mary, she thinks we are nothing," Lilly had heard her mother say, in tears. Lilly had tried to console Helen. Her mother had carried a hunger like Lilly felt now in the baptistery, something insatiable and off-limits, too. It hadn't shamed Helen as it shamed Lilly now, to feel such overwhelming appetite for the love of the nurturing figure who was all powerful. Now in the baptistery, years later, Lilly felt painfully empty. *Only this little boy on Mother Mary's lap was loved*, Lilly thought, as she found herself yearning to fall into oblivious sleep on the lap of the Mother Mary statue whose arms—strong and loving—had no animal raw body underneath the pure white gown. Lilly could not bear this, a lust to be loved so ideally and completely. Her mother was incomplete, she thought, searching and starving, and Lilly was born from a hungry, wandering womb.

The baptistery was humid and sultry, as one of those sordid bathhouses in the East Village where male strangers went to copulate, men on men. The windows sweated, and Lilly felt as though she were in a tomb and a bathhouse all at once.

Death and water filled her dreams later that night. She found herself imagining she was a young boy and a part of this elevated rite of passage, and then her dreams began to disturb and terrify her.

The bulb became turbulence within her, a threat of nightmare confusions.

Lilly avoided the baptistery. She tried to sleep late, and after she heard Jane leave the apartment for somewhere else, Lilly gathered herself up for no reason but to wash and eat something and return to her room to try to write and read one of her schoolbooks—not so much to study, or to write coherently, but to wait for something to happen to pull her out of living this way.

The snows cleared, and the school reopened. One late February afternoon Lilly decided to try going back to her classes at Sarah Lawrence. She returned to the college but could not go to the seminar rooms and classrooms.

That same evening, she didn't take the train back to the city, spending her supper money on three Mars bars from the vending machines in the library basement. Her head was filled with darkness, and she felt frightened to return to Little Italy—the apartment with its memories of being unable to hold onto Mitchell, Jane's threatening warmth, and the images in the baptistery.

The temperature was dropping; she saw it in the little red dial on the thermostats inside the library building. Outside the wide window, the vast, whitened blur of campus buildings and trees collected more ominous signs of the forbidding cold.

Lilly took the spiral stairway up to the library's third floor.

Scattered books were sprawled haphazardly on different wheeled conveyances in the hall. Some were lying on their sides, not yet catalogued. There were three such dollies jammed with course books, thick texts from a hundred courses Lilly didn't know about.

At first, she thought she was drawn to the books because she recognized the same religious symbols she had seen in the baptistery; figures of deacons, lustrous crowns, and crosses.

Slowly, she advanced through the stack.

Lilly was warm when she carried the books into a study room filled with enormous pillows and study areas with desks and lamps. Forty or so gigantic pillows were laid down to make a floor that could be utilized to lie, sit, and study on through the night. Lilly stumbled through the field of pillows with one of the thick volumes.

Alchemy and Hermetic Philosophy: A Brief Overview of Alchemy . . . she started reading as she let herself sink into a nest of floor pillows.

> The alchemical tradition came from the earlier practitioners of the "spagyric" science . . . (from Greek *spaein*—to rend, tear apart—and *ageirein*—to bring together) and claimed matter as both the source of their wisdom and the salvation of their soul's desire. The Egyptian goddess, Isis, was said to be the founder of alchemy. However, the science probably originated with the women who used the chemical processes to formulate perfumes and cosmetics in ancient Mesopotamia.

Similarly, Babylonian women chemists used recipes and equipment derived from the kitchen. Thus, ancient alchemy was identified with women, and the work of the early alchemists occasionally was referred to as *opus mulierum*, or "women's work."

There were drawings, too, of symbols and the body—bones and genitals. A transforming furnace known as the "Athanor" was a kiln with adorned nipples at its upper part. There were also charcoal-black etchings in the book, of figures neither male nor female but created with ambiguous genitalia—males spawned large oval eggs, dropping from penises like sacs; the pubes of women sprouted rods and long snakes. Hermaphrodites possessed acacias for genitals that shot up with pulp red flowers into the heavens. Symbols of citadels with towers prevailed on the pages, as did drawbridges over long and wavy rivers, hawks, green lions, lambs, and people with yellow solar faces and skulls.

The entire opus was steeped in confounding symbols, a combination of real chemical reactions with the alchemist's own projections. In the pictorial language of the alchemists, "Trees grew between the legs . . . and phalluses and royal peacocks, the royal marriage of the king and queen took place. . . ." It was known that the fumes from heated mercury could induce orgasms in the alchemist's body that were not literal, but hallucinatory, the properties of the alchemist merged with those from the substances burning in the furnace.

> The alchemist, explained the books, could no lon-
> ger tell "the psychically real from the physically
> real, they were one and the same to the alche-
> mist . . . They [the orgasms] are recognized for
> what they are only much later, if ever. Secrecy is
> essential."

She had only been in the pillow room an hour before she felt a shock as she recognized the same bizarre symbols and illustrations she once saw in the texts on her mother's bookbinding table. There was no mistaking some of the etchings: spheres of fire and wind, gold painted animals, birds, and naked figures called "the bibliotheca hebraea" in these alchemy books. Helen was there powerfully with her in the task and the subject.

"It began like this," she would write in her first alchemy notebook that same night, when she found her own words. And then as she wrote, the moments in the bathtub during the night of her father's accident began to come back to her. She described the bathroom window she had looked out, waiting for her mother to return that evening, the sounds of the old pipes. She heard the thud again below her and felt her mind go blank as it had in the bathtub that night. She remembered the intense pleasure she had in the water, and she felt her old confusion, groping again for something that might explain why she had ignored the warning that her father had fallen again, something to show her she wasn't to blame for her father's coma. But again she was enveloped by the amnesiac haze. Guilt seized her again, and an anguished shame.

"Something worthless can be burnished into gold," Lilly read from one of the texts, imagining herself burnishing as one of the crude metals personified in the text, setting a fire in which she would burn as both arsonist and arsonist's victim. And then, nobody would be destroyed but her, she thought.

Filled and embraced as if the books had souls, Lilly searched and found the bulb in different alchemy books.

The bulb between a naked woman's legs was in one of the illustrations made by Maria the Jewess from Babylon in the second century. Finding it, Lilly felt her body lighten as if she had crossed through the barrier of her shame. *There were other women like this*, she thought. Like *her*.

One of the books described the bulb as "a consolidated nucleus of the personality which can appear to the alchemist as symbols, shadows like the philosophic trees that spring from the phalluses of the androgens, from Saturn and Venus . . ."

That night, Lilly's own bulb returned, less frightening and disturbing. She felt it nestled firmly between her thighs.

By around midnight, Lilly heard the student librarian below calling up the stairway, asking if anyone were left in the library. Hearing nothing, the girl locked up the building and it was completely dark. Lilly waited and then turned one study light on in the pillow room.

The room was soft and private. She gathered the texts, piled them on the floor so that they looked like square rocks resting on the waves of a sea of pillows in the room. Helen was there in her mind, along with the skeins of leather her mother hung in the basement workroom when Lilly was a child. Throbbing with a delicious loneliness, she caught herself wondering if Helen felt like this in the basement, a foreigner except for the hours she spent bookbinding.

By morning, Lilly read through more than eleven texts, and the real world had become unreal again. The pictures and images she saw in the etchings in the alchemy books became a formulating guide to her madness. She would arrive at something meaningful, she told herself. She could become an outside investigator of the mysterious bulb, her labile states between reality and unreality—observing an exemplary case of madness in a long history of fathomless depths. She would document the history in her notebooks. It belonged only to that world of alchemy and ancient texts. Lilly carefully put all the alchemy books back on the dolly and then washed herself in the bathroom in the basement. She entered the outside by prying open a window before the librarians came back to the building.

She went back to Manhattan; Jane wasn't there when she returned to the apartment. She went into the empty kitchen. Mitchell had left a lint cloth on the counter weeks ago, the one he cleaned his violin with, and now she picked it up and dropped it into a garbage pail.

Lilly missed school again that morning. The Little Italy streets were deserted when she looked out her bedroom window a few hours later. Undressing, she slipped naked between the sheets in exhaustion. But she was feeling the bulb. She wouldn't answer the phone if the school called, if anyone called, she promised herself. Before she let herself drift into sleep, she planned how she was going to spread out all her mimeographed pages of notes about alchemy on the old wobbly desk she had barely used before this day. She would include the characters who had come to her in the library. She could, maybe, propose to her college don a thesis on alchemy, to keep her place in the college. It felt hopeful before she fell off into the dark state that came with sleep. Then Lilly was drowning; the alchemy, too, was failing her. In the dreams, blended into shocks and images, she saw androgynous figurines drifting from the alchemy texts, and she was floating up to join them as they mirrored her freakishness.

What had gone wrong? Lilly asked herself now in the seclusion room of the hospital.

How was it possible for Lilly to feel alone and crazy when there were pages and pages filled with voyagers of the self like her, centuries of them, packed as if in a telephone book full of phone numbers she could make calls to in her despair? How was it possible to feel hopelessness when despair itself "facilitated a unification of the limited with the unlimited," as the books explained?

In spite of everything she wrote in the day, the dreams and the confusions came back in the night. She had lost control. In only a few weeks, her writing slid away from her.

₪

Now she felt like a slap the stark white loneliness of the seclusion room.

Lilly took in a thickening breath; she did not want tears. She looked for her crushed pack of Marlboros in the quiet room, but they had taken them away along with her matches. Instead, she struggled to concentrate. She needed to piece together just the last long hours, the drive in the taxicab with Jane, the procedure in the emergency room, and what had happened to her in the examination.

But within seconds she imagined Dr. Burkert moving under the sheets with her, and then his long hands spanking her thighs. The bulb was growing again. She felt it pulse, swelling her with that familiar fear. How complete was her helplessness against that sudden moment's visitation from a deep and awful eros.

No, she couldn't permit this. To come here? Into a mental hospital? Like some wild element from an archaic chart of chemicals and compounds let loose upon the real world?

Lilly wished she had a match that she could ignite and touch its fire to her skin.

The fire could singe a tiny spot on her flesh that would send flashes of pain throughout her body, driving out the hot flush in the bulb. Anything to obliterate the fire within her. Inside Lilly was a place where blood was flowing wildly as mercury in the chaotic heat of her flesh. It made her eyes close, and then she only wanted to lose herself.

She tried to lie still. If she looked too distressed by what was happening in her body, her sex, Dr. Burkert or the cold nurse would soon notice the bulb when they came back into the room.

"Mercury must be baked in a triple receptacle of very hard glass." She forced herself to remember something said in her alchemy texts. Her feelings could be contained, she told herself, make sense again. She told herself not to panic. She would understand everything that was happening. Soon. When her mind was clearer. She would just have to be patient, and her sense and logic would come back.

Lilly tightened the belt of her gown. Where were her writings? And all her plans and notes? There would be questions— from the college, from her mother about what happened to her. So she must retain control. She would be mad and unmad.

She had to stay here. There were darker houses for the genuinely crazy than this mental hospital, and people who were totally insane. She must not become unhinged or look disturbed. And she could not fall, crash, or skid—hurt herself in any way so that they would have take care of her. She didn't want any real person to take care of her.

The quiet room resembled a basement. Why shouldn't she stay here?

She needed a strategy. She must avoid the nurse. This was the first rule she set for herself. If she were to survive this journey, she must stay away from Beverly.

Slowly Lilly rolled from her side onto her back. She sank deeper into the mattress. She stared up at the peels and flakes of white on the ceiling.

Lilly felt her heart beating in her ear. Then she remembered she had forgotten to shut the window in her apartment. It was open, and the wind had been so strong the past few days.

Could it have blown all her notes away?

Chapter Four

"Please find a seat," said a thickset nurse, sitting in the closest chair to the open corridor. "You need to take a seat before we begin. I understand this is your first community meeting." She quickly glanced down at a clipboard of ruffled notes and patients' names on her knees. "This is Lillian, everybody." The nurse's ruddy face was too uplifting in the bleak silence of the room. Her hair was in a rumpled bun, loose hanks splashing across her forehead as she looked back up and around the circle. Except for the chain of passkeys hanging from her belt, she did not seem like the other nurses. She was wearing cherry-brown loafers that matched her masculine, wide-lapelled shirt. A plain denim skirt aproned her chubby lap. "Lillian, you can't stand during a community meeting," she said again. "There's a chair by Lisa."

The hospital shifts had changed. Lilly was released from the quiet room by 8 p.m. A nurse had come, taking her from the quiet room to a private room on the hall.

Now Lilly felt alert. The medicine of hours ago had almost finished its watch over her impulses and quelled her. She moved hesitantly amid the hive of new faces and bodies. As in an airport where a flight was interminably delayed, all the patients looked stranded and anxious in the surroundings of ashtrays, magazine racks, and game tables where Scrabble and backgammon boards were folded away for the meeting.

"Lillian, I'm Caroline," the same nurse said to Lilly. "We haven't met yet. Okay. Everyone's here."

"Where's Spia?" a young female patient asked. "Is Spia back in the quiet room, Caroline?"

Caroline turned to an aide. "You better go find her," she said to him.

The aide disappeared down the long corridor as Lilly sat down next to a heavily freckled, thin young woman she guessed was Lisa.

Spia arrived from the other side of the hall in a pair of frilly green panties showing through her thrift-shop negligee. She carried two stuffed brown grocery bags.

"Oh, Spia," Lisa said. "Why're you doing this?"

"I'm leaving after the meeting," Spia said in a gruff Haitian accent. "I'm going back to dancing. I'm going to dance at the club tonight. They're already sold out for my show." She plopped into a chair, pulled at the negligee that was too short and tight for her muscular body, and leered at Caroline.

"We will all be helping Spia if we simply do not pay any attention to this," Caroline said. "I ask you, as a community, to please not look at Spia right now."

"That's a little hard, isn't it?" a male patient laughed.

"I can't understand what you find so goddamn funny," another male patient said. "My bedroom happens to be right next to the quiet room where she was screaming her head off all morning. If she can't keep her mouth shut, why don't you lock her up someplace else, Caroline?"

"Well, Tom, I can see that Spia has aroused some very strong feelings in you."

"Dammit, Caroline! I'm taking a shower, and she comes waltzing in. Every time you let her out of the quiet room she's doing something."

Caroline looked at Spia. "Spia? Did you walk into Tom's shower?"

Spia nodded.

"Perhaps you'd like to say something to Tom, Spia. You've made him very angry."

Spia smiled. "I love you, Tom," she said. "I love everyone here."

"All right, I think it would be best if we dropped the matter for now." Caroline picked a fallen hair out of her mouth. "Tom, I suggest you talk to Dr. Leach about your feelings. I'd like to start the meeting now. Lisa, please read the minutes from the last week so we can begin."

The woman called Lisa shuffled a stack of loose-leaf pages on her lap. She was about twenty. Her freckled face and angular head looked too large for her squat body. She was wearing a corduroy jumper that Lilly had seen in junior high school, on the physically shy girls. After rolling her tongue over her freckled lips, she read,

April 10th, 1974. Tom said he couldn't stand the way the place was overheated anymore. Caroline said he'd have to; it was an old building and nothing could be done. Tom said: Why couldn't some of the patients go sunbathe on the roof instead of going to recreational therapy since the weather was finally getting nice? Caroline said no. Tom asked if there could be a volleyball game on Wednesday night, and Caroline said she would look into this; the adolescents had the gym then. Sister Emelda asked if anybody knew whether Patty Hearst had been caught yet, and Sophie said the F.B.I. was in her bedroom all the time. Tom said he was sick of living with crazy people all the time. Louise Whitty said Spia was a thief, too; she had stolen three boxes of caramel Ayds from her because she was running low, it wasn't fair. Spia said you can stuff your Ayds up your fat ass, they don't taste good anyway. Louise Whitty began to cry. Spia began to cry too. . . .

The air filled with sounds of restlessness, bottoms squeaking against the wooden seats of their chairs. It smelled like smoke, fresh Lemon Pledge, mahogany, polished floors. The fresh clouds the patients blew from their cigarettes mingled with the lasting odors of a steak and mashed potatoes dinner still wafting in from the dining room.

Lilly sucked in tiny, quick breaths. She tried to keep her eyes on the floor, but felt them drawn to the faces around her. The real world of the hospital was coming to life faster than she could endure.

As Lisa read the long pages of detailed minutes, Lilly watched Spia sitting with her legs apart, smiling complacently as she captured eyes. Spia was leaning back into her chair and rolling her hips, aiming her laced crotch at Caroline.

Next to Spia, a nun was strapped in a chair, a white canvas harness around her pudgy torso, a pristine child. While Spia thrashed around beside her, the nun's face remained serene.

Lilly felt inside her jeans for the pack of Viceroys, but then she remembered she had dropped them in a drawer in her new room. She began to blink rapidly, to stay alert. She sensed the others staring at her, but she would not give into her trembling. She crossed her legs on her chair seat, and she felt an immense slack in her blue jeans, as if she had lost pounds just in the three hours she spent in the quiet room. Then she imagined the emptiness she would feel if she were back in the apartment in Little

Italy. She envisioned herself not returning to her apartment, not having to return anywhere, unburdened, her former life vaporized, expunged. She was still anonymous here, and though she felt the desperation of the others around her, there was relief in knowing it wasn't her own desperation.

The window was opened half an inch, and Lilly heard the rain spraying down into the leaves below the ledge. It hissed like a baby peeing into soft blankets. And, listening to it, Lilly was suddenly floating in a dissolution of space, a gust of thrill, foreign and exciting. She felt the pull of her own madness, the bulb, the confusing currents washing alternately through her and her fantasy world, like running water, merging the real world and this other realm that she needed time to comprehend.

Something had happened to her and it took along her body, its meaning locked within herself. She felt a refuge in the swelling mass of others and their suffering. She could lose herself here, hide while she found herself, if only for a short time.

Lisa laid the rumpled loose-leaf pages of minutes under her chair and looked up at Caroline, mashing her lips together.

"Thank you for reading the minutes, Lisa," Caroline said. "Would anyone like to comment? Are there any new issues people have this evening? Leonard, perhaps you'd like to share with the group how it feels to be going out to the outside world tomorrow?"

"No thanks." Leonard dropped the *Time* magazine he had been reading instead of listening to Lisa's notes. He did not look straight at anyone. His lap was thick, his thighs muscular.

"Leonard will be downtown at City Hall in the mornings starting Tuesday for his trial," Caroline announced to the group.

"Don't you worry about it," Leonard said. Next to Leonard, a thin man sat, in strong contrast to Leonard's bulk. His weak hands were veiny, and he wore a boy's baseball cap, a royal blue classic with the Mets crest embroidered on it in gold wool threads. But even the hypermasculine hat failed to add much to his slight form. The man's eyes were dark and blank in their holes. He wore no socks, and his Hush Puppies shoes looked girlish. His figure barely threw a shadow on the wall. His fingers drummed on his Gap jeans.

"Arnold, would you like to share with the community what you're feeling?" Caroline asked him.

Arnold waved his hand "no" angrily at her.

"Do people want to say something to Arnold?" Caroline asked the silent circle.

Lilly moved uncomfortably in her seat. Caroline's warmth was a sneaky seduction, Lilly thought. She would be careful of Caroline.

"I don't much appreciate what's happening to me either, Arnold," Leonard said. His hand jetted down to his trouser pocket, taking out a gold-plated lighter. When he flicked it, the flame was tall and blazing. He leaned into the fire; his face almost touched it.

In one of his pockets was an old but stylish tie, *a Gucci*, Lilly thought, *or an Yves St. Laurent, or some other designer.* Leonard clapped the lid of his lighter shut, stoking on his lit cigarette. Then his left hand returned the lighter to his pocket, and he looked more in command of himself again.

"Leonard, would you like to share with the group how you are feeling about going down to the courthouse tomorrow?" Caroline asked him.

"Nope," Leonard said, and smiled at her.

There was a long silence.

A sharp ringing began in Lilly's ear. Her head swelled with the delible faces and figures of the patients. An internal camera was developing its film in her own private darkroom now.

"You're beautiful, Caroline," a large female patient blurted.

"Thank you," Caroline said. "But Louise, do you have anything to say to the group?"

"You're a Rodin woman, honey. I miss the times when there were women of mystery." Louise pulled at her dress, a flowing faux silvery-sequined lounge gown. Her hair was like a Clorox-soaked broom head, its yellow straw ends stiff and spiky. A colorful feather boa straddled her neck. "Did you know Marilyn Monroe was hospitalized here?" she asked. "See what I mean? Women can do this 'crazy' role better because we are submissive and helpless and we can have *crisis. Crisis* isn't so bad. Crisis and pain and despair take you into being a whole person. It's about what's existential," Louise finished. "But it's also about orgasms."

"Jesus Christ, Louise," Lisa said.

"All right, Louise and Lisa," Caroline said. "Let's stay focused."

Lilly startled. She struggled to stop the bulb from coming to life; she tried hard not to listen, to dampen its fire.

There were creaks and sighs, some loose jokes, and more bantering. The half an hour was passing quickly. Caroline's gaze rested one by one on each patient, as if to make sure she didn't miss any gesture, any mutter.

The patients in the room soon seemed to have taken on a family resemblance, patches of paleness on their skin under stiff, gaudy clothing.

"If you all don't quit yakking," Spia hissed into the noisy room, "I gonna walk out of here. You all sick in the head."

But by now Lilly realized the meeting was breaking up. Two nurses were calling out from down the corridor, "Meds are ready!" Patients were standing, pulling their chairs back. A black aide started turning on the three standing lamps to signal that the meeting was officially over. And then a chaotic dispersal of energy was unleashed in the changing light.

Lilly stayed seated. She watched Caroline. The nurse was standing now, directing the patients to clear out of the center lounge. There was a loud shuffling of armchairs under all the lights, which had been turned on so brightly as the meeting was ending.

Sucking in the smoke-saturated air, Lilly needed to get up now, to walk in the aimless trajectory of the other patients, pacing back and forth, between the north and south sides, or sitting at the TV in the other lounge, at the game tables, on the faux leather couches, listening to the night roars of traffic on the FDR Drive out the windows.

Lilly looked around in the room's commotion to see whether one of the aides or nurses was waiting for her, to take her back to her room. But no one seemed to be noticing her now. She looked up at the clock. Nine-thirty, she read from the Victorian antique grandfather clock standing between the game table and the armchair in the lounge.

She wondered what the distance was between the center lounge and the private room she had been given. She would measure it soon; it would be something to do to pass the time. She would have to find something to fill the time here, which she knew now would be long.

₪

"Hello, Mom?" It was 10 p.m. when Lilly got to the phone booth.

"Lilly! Oh, thank God! What is going on? Why didn't you call earlier?"

"I've been sort of busy."

"What happened? I called the apartment, and Jane said you went into a mental hospital. It was a horrible way for me to find out, Lilly. Why didn't you call me?"

"I'm calling you now, Mom."

"I don't understand, Lillian. What does that girl Jane know? She knows nothing, too." Helen was slipping into her

Israeli accent, her voice growing frantic. "This girl Jane doesn't know what happened to you. Who is this girl? You know her from school?"

"Yes, Mom."

"Why are you being so cruel to me, Lillian? Why do you do things like this?"

"I'm not being cruel," Lilly said.

"Yes, you are very cruel, Lillian. Not even telling me you are in trouble. You are trying to punish all of us, aren't you, little girl?"

"Mom—"

"I spoke to your doctor. How old is he? Is he married?"

"I really didn't ask."

"He said you weren't telling him anything either. I don't understand, Lillian. What are you trying to do to me?"

"Look, I'm fine. I'm not going to be here much longer."

"But why are you there at all? Did you eat sugar, Lillian? I told you your body cannot take sugar in the food. Is there sugar in what they feed you there? Don't touch it, you hear me? It can make you act this way. I read this in a magazine."

"I'm not here because I ate sugar."

"Then why? Why are you there?"

"As I said, it's not for very long."

"You are not going to tell anyone? If you can't tell me, you can tell that doctor. What did I ever do that makes you act like this to me? You are the one that did this to me, Lilly."

"It has nothing to do with you."

"Is it your father?"

"I don't know what you're talking about."

"I know. It's not the sugar. I know what is happening to us, Lilly. You are sorry for what you did to me. It doesn't mean for you to suffer. It does not mean for you to go into a mental hospital."

"I have to go now, Mom."

"Lilly, listen to me. He's a sick man. He didn't call you again, did he?"

"Mom, I'm in a hospital—"

"There is nothing to do for him. I already told you your father can't be put in a hospital. It is brain damage that he has and no one can fix him, Lilly. You haven't heard this enough?"

"I have to go now, Mom—"

"Let me come there and help you with this. Darling, I want to come. Let me come—"

Lilly let the receiver drop. Then she pulled up the coiled cord and slammed the receiver back into its cradle.

Lilly bumped her way down the corridor through a flow of staring faces. The door of the phone booth was still swinging as she moved, tightening her lips into the most completely formed smile she could make. But she had to stay composed. She had to.

Finally, she turned inside the opened door of her room through its threshold. Into safety.

₪

In her hospital room, Lilly lifted her T-shirt and pulled it up, off her neck.

She tried to shake off her thoughts as she finished undressing. Lilly missed her alchemy books and her notebooks.

Lilly's room was spare and simple, like a 1920s hotel room on Gramercy Park—all chestnut and rosewood and tranquil beauty. Just a lovely bureau, a bed, a small braided rug on the wooden floor, and then a small writing table by the window. The walls were bare, but polished and pure as white enamel.

In the corner—as was the case with old rooms constructed long ago—was a small washing sink, along with a tiny bar of olive-colored soap and two wash towels hanging neatly on a brass ring under the sink.

Even after Jane and she scrubbed the cracked tile and plaster floors, the Little Italy apartment was mildewed. The hallway of their slum tenement in Little Italy smelled of cats and bacon. The bums camping inside it stretched on newspapers for bedding, on the cracked Florentine tiles of the hallways.

Now a filled shopping bag was perched against the clean hospital room's closet door. She recognized Jane's handwriting on a note Scotch taped on the bag. Lilly found the plain blue nightshirt Jane had stuffed into the bag with other unfolded, random clothes, and she pulled the nightshirt out. Then she let it drape on her. Somehow it had maintained its light but certain shape inside the messy spill of the bag.

Lilly tried to get ready to go to sleep. She folded her dirty blue jeans and T-shirt. Then she pushed her worn panties into a plastic bag provided for laundry, and she put it inside the closet. She opened the paper-lined bureau drawers and started putting the clothes Jane had packed inside them, folding, arranging them until the shopping bag was finally empty.

She was here now, Lilly thought, surrounded by polished corridors, soft yellow lamplight, and settees, in a clean hospital room filled with expensive furnishings. Every hope she had left was in this hospital, this room.

There could be refuge here. And maybe the states would get better so she could write again. She hadn't been able to write anything for so long.

"This is called the Salt of Alchemy," Lilly remembered the text inside an alchemy book. "The Salt is divided into fixed Salt and volatile Salt. . . ."

She wanted to stay here in the hospital, where people couldn't swallow her, she thought, or ignite her into flames and ash. She just wanted to be able to write in her notebook again, to feel the lightness she used to feel when she packed the outside world up and put it away somewhere so it couldn't hurt her anymore.

Chapter Five

Two weeks before, Lilly had taken the 10:30 a.m. off-peak train out of Grand Central and visited her parents for the last time. Glints of sun had speared through the train compartment, shimmered. The stations out her window had seemed like visual echoes as the train clipped past them. "White Plains, North White Plains, Valhalla . . ."

Three students were on the opposite aisle, smelling of cheap wine and the packages of trail mix they still held opened on their laps. She used to be them, she thought, once riding the train from Bedford to the city, without a care. Now there was no worse place to be than rolling through the same beautiful Westchester hills, remembering herself in other faces.

Outside the train window, Lilly had watched the starched white houses of the wealthy Westchester suburbs pass, thinking that everything inside her other world before her father's accident was not real: the old school dresses her mother picked out for her and the curtains over the colonial windows, the night sounds of her mother and father sleeping in their bedroom upstairs, the birthing dusks of Bedford and the hours she could make the world of attachments fall away.

Her past life had seemed a muddle, a clutter; feelings were all mixed up in it. It was still her life in her dreams and in waking life when she remembered something that happened—a place or a person—but she had to strain to identify what or whom.

Faint newspaper prints were on the inside of her father's thumb when Lilly saw him in her memory sometimes before his accident, and he was walking to catch the train home in her recollections, passing the Roosevelt Hotel on Fortieth Street, walking through a long inside passageway filled with shoeshine stands and newspaper stands in Grand Central Station, a tiny curl of black and gray hair under his felt hat, the newspaper under his arm that he would fold, column by column, like beautiful pressed leaves, on the New York Central railroad train seat. His journals of *Commentary* and the *Columbia University Law Review* were piled up on the sill of his office in New York City with Broadway theater *Playbill*s: *She Loves Me, Camelot, Oliver!* . . . Broadway theater marquees were visible and glittering through its dingy glass windows.

"Do you want something more, sweetheart?" he asked her once when she accompanied him through the bronze-gilded building on Fifth Avenue. His office was on the thirty-fifth floor, and she was playing with the water cooler, pressing the tap up and down to watch the water bubble inside the glass tank. "How about a date? Will you go with me to the Cattleman? We'll make a treat out of it." His question had come after a long silence. He had been staring at her as she was flapping the tap up and down, the water spilling onto his beige and pink marble floor. Lilly was a small girl for her age then, eleven years old.

Under the sultry light, the piano bar in the Cattleman had looked like a mahogany pool. He did not tell her the young actress would be waiting for him, by the coat check. The actress had simply emerged in the dim light, her hair unpinned, her eyelashes like miniature tents. Ushered to a table through the half-empty dining room, her father had sat under a painting of a cowboy riding a bucking horse—the cowboy was whip-ping a lasso out into the sky. The actress, following him, took the seat directly opposite him so that Lilly was left to the side seat where there was no place setting laid for a third diner. The actress took a file out of her purse and began to file her thumb-nails, waiting for the menus. David threw his own cloth napkin across his lap. He had straightened the manila folder of a con-tract and fingered the sharpened no. 2 pencils he drew from his attaché case. He put on his half-glasses and drummed a pencil on the folder. By then he had forgotten Lilly.

They were never beautiful, the "girls," as he called them, the clients from Broadway shows, or TV situation comedies, or movies in Los Angeles. They looked foolish against his long, in-telligent face, his hypercritical eyes, and he did not have affairs with them, Lilly believed, resenting the opulent show he put on around the actress that evening. She was filling with the un-comfortable mix of feelings she had for her father, a part of her wanting to spurn everything around him, wanting her mother to return. She could walk out into the anonymous bustle and traffic of the city, she had thought. The fragrance of cognac and liqueurs from the bar wafted through the restaurant air, and even her glass of Coca-Cola seemed—like her father—extrava-gant, a little reckless and grand. She would resist him, but she could not hate him.

Toward her father, Lilly could not remember when she didn't feel resentment and emptiness. That abyss was unbear-able, a hole within her he refused to assert his will enough to fill, charming her playfully as he neglected her—a rattlesnake dance over the fire of desires. The pushing desperation for his attention, she remembered it all now on the train, but had she wanted to harm him? Is that why she had left him on the floor that night of the accident? What secret did her amnesia about what really happened that night, three years ago, protect her from ever knowing?

Whatever her father did before his accident seemed to Lilly mysterious, too. The way her mother and she both had to wait for him to finish his dinner most evenings. Watching him butter his bread with soft, imported Danish cheeses and gaze at the lawn or the swimming pool down the driveway, and then suddenly turn back to notice what both of them were wearing, a dress or slacks. Perusing their legs with one of his eyebrows raised. There were large, gold-sculpted cigar humidifiers on her father's mahogany desk in his study, along with racks of meerschaum and virgin briar pipes and his closet full of his stylish attorneys' tweed and gray flannel suits that he wore to his successful entertainment law practice in the city. David was medium-height with a long nose and thin, quiet lips. His chest was wide. His attractive arms—athletic and strong. But he had been as remote and ethereal as the granite Bedford cliffs and the woods.

On her train seat that last visit home, Lilly drew out two letters she had pulled from her desk drawer before she left the apartment in Little Italy. She read again:

Re: David Weill.

Dear Dr. Spiegal,

. . . As per your request for more background on Mr. Weill, we are sending you a copy of our findings and the discharge summary on this patient from June 15, 1971. Copies of this letter have been sent to Mrs. Weill at her Westchester address. As we stated previously, the original medical summary was sent to Dr. Sacci at the time the patient was discharged into his care three years ago.

Lilly had been keeping the letter to give to her mother, received in the day's mail when she took her father in for a checkup at the local medical center a few weeks ago. Some voice inside her told her that Helen would lose it in the stack of papers her mother now continually mishandled, piles on top of the dusty desk in her father's study off the master bedroom. Helen tossed mail there now that she didn't open for days, sometimes weeks. The neglected bulk of mail got mixed in with all unopened subscription magazines and other sundry mail packets in tall, thick, unsorted batches. Lilly had meant to tell her mother about it that evening weeks ago. Then Lilly just kept the letter to herself.

She continued reading:

> It seems possible at this point to assume that Mr. Weill had a stroke at the top of the stairway which made him fall, or perhaps he lost his footing for another reason, and suffered a cerebral insult in his fall. However, it seems more clear that he suffered a stroke, possibly another stroke in the kitchen which rendered him unconscious for several hours until his wife found him.
>
> His daughter reported in several interviews with our neurologists here that her memory of this night is vague. She went out of her bedroom to check if Mr. Weill were all right after she heard his initial fall, but she cannot remember if she heard his second fall in the kitchen. She was still upstairs. Mrs. Weill walked into the kitchen an hour later and found him.

Mr. Weill was known to complain of migraines and there were noted stress factors, both psychologically and medically that contributed to his emotional and physical state.

Unfortunately, the insurance situation does present a problem for future care here in the rehabilitation unit. We understand that Mr. Weill had been planning to change his insurance plan but since he was in the process of completing divorce proceedings with his wife, he did not attend to this before his strokes, and he currently has no coverage. We have, of course, tried to bring this to the attention of social services but it has not yielded positive results. Regardless of Mr. Weill's intentions before his illness, the legal documents would be necessary. Therefore, I'm afraid our department can no longer accommodate Mr. Weill's medical needs. However, we are guarded in our opinion as to an effective rehabilitative treatment for Mr. Weill's condition regardless of his financial situation. Recommendations for several home nursing services were given to Mrs. Weill who has, to my knowledge, procured some employment to pay for her husband's long stay as an inpatient in Northern Westchester Hospital.

Regrettably, the cerebral insult Mr. Weill suffered as a result of his two strokes and accident on the stairs was diffuse, bilateral, and resulted in significant forebrain injury. Upon awakening from the coma, he appeared to have undergone a dramatic personality change as well as a loosening of affect and inhibition in the hospital, causing much inappropriate behavior on his part. Rage and severe agitation were notable. Loose and uninhibited sexual behavior have also been observed, along with occasional flights of fancy and depression.

The staff here at Northern Westchester Medical Center was not surprised to hear the summary of Mr. Weill's gradual deterioration these three years. After two months' hospitalization here, the patient was well enough to be sent home but he continued to exhibit curious fits of anger and violence, a short attention span, impaired memory, perseveration of word and act, extreme personality change, uninhibited sexual behavior, salivary drooling and urinary dribbling.

Neurological examination had showed a blood pressure of 200/100. He exhibited a slow spastic gait. He also exhibited a defect of revisualization and conceptualization since he was unable to draw the face of a clock or reproduce a simple floor plan of his own home or even of his bedroom.

Librium was prescribed 10 mg four times a day. However the prognosis for Mr. Weill remains guarded. It was certain at this time that Mr. Weill would not be able to return to his law practice or any other form of his previous employment.

However, as stated earlier, without sufficient insurance, we cannot refer this case to our team here, and social services has explained future referrals can only be made if bankruptcy is declared which Mrs. Weill will not agree to. Her college-age daughter also doesn't qualify for Medicaid benefits, as she is no longer a minor, and the family was well above the income level for welfare.

We hope that this letter will be useful in understanding the complications in this case.

Thank you for letting us share this interesting problem with you.

Sincerely,
Dr. Morton Vesell
Rehabilitation Unit
Northern Westchester Hospital

Lilly folded the first letter, taking out from the same envelope another letter that Helen had written her from a Mind Dynamics retreat in Connecticut a few days ago, urging her to come home:

Lilly, my darling, I am coming home tomorrow. The people are very nice to me here. I will need you to come again to watch your father this Sunday. I must go to work this day because I have been away. In summer, perhaps it will be different, perhaps he will be well at last. Tell the tuition people not to call me at work, please. I will pay when I can. I'm sending you the check for the rent now. We both must try to keep up our appearances, no matter what the money situation is, darling. I have always looked nice. Next time, why don't we go to the retreat together and get positive energy?

I know someday you will understand how much your mother has suffered with this man in the house. Let him sit in his room and watch the t.v. all day. He's a baby, that's the whole problem with this man and even before this he was a baby. He likes to ruin everything. Hate me if it makes you feel better, if you have less guilt for causing all this to happen to me.

I'm not trying to ruin your life, I have let you have your own apartment, haven't I?

Love,
Your Mommy

Lilly folded the letters back into the envelope and put them under her Marlboro cigarettes, in the bottom scatter of the purse.

These past long months, the Bedford house was quiet with the tragic steps of her father holding onto his aluminum walker as he struggled to walk and move. When David came home from the hospital three years before, her mother moved him out of their bedroom into the mudroom—an extra guest room off the kitchen, with an old Magnavox TV, boxes of discarded clothes meant to be delivered to some charity or finally thrown away, and a bed that still smelled like the litter of puppies the dog had given birth to years ago. Not an unpleasant odor, but it wasn't human. Upstairs, her mother's part of the bedroom was messy, and there were drawers of nylons and girdles left pulled open in the dressers. Helen went to work at a small travel agency called Directions Unlimited. And Helen stopped her bookbinding. She received discount miles and hotel rates and left the house for "business trips." Soon, Helen didn't want to pay anymore for David's private nurse. Besides, the money was running out. There was no insurance to help pay. And they were not covered for the months her father spent in the hospital. Tuition installments and Lilly's rent were always late. Lilly was worried she would have to leave Sarah Lawrence and live at home again.

Fifty-five years old when it happened, her father kept reminding Lilly, and not time enough to prepare for disaster.

The tears are rolling down his cheeks, Lilly had thought on
the train that morning. Even here, as she sat on the train and
waited for her stop, she could hear her father's thoughts. *Where
is Helen, where is your mother? It's not snowing, but the roads are
dangerous. Where's Helen?* Lilly could hear him as if he were inside her and his thoughts were hers. Something in these three
years since his strokes manipulated that, and now she was a
medium for her father. She knew her father was walking with
his aluminum walker into the living room right now, and that
the sun was coming through the oval windows of the colonial
house. *Will your mother come home?* he will ask her when she arrives, Lilly thought, then he will wait for Lilly to answer him.
*Has there been an accident? My brother Leon talks to me at night
in dreams, and I have no will to live. I want to write my story. It
would make a great novel*, he will tell her. *Helen was a dish when I
first met her. . . . Oh boy, we were wild. Lilly, you are my confidante
now and dearest girl. How did I manage all these years?* Could Lilly show him how to write his novel? She's the one in the family
who writes all the time. Would Lilly help him tell his story?

When David possessed Lilly, it was through her whole
body, and she couldn't stop the flow of her father into her. A
brain-damaged man cannot speak his mind; he must go through
someone else. *It closes in on them, the house. A brain-damaged
man exposes all his secrets. And I can hear inside my father,* Lilly
thought. She wondered how much water her father must drink
to make so many tears. *Joe and Larry were his good friends*, he is
thinking now. . . . And when he thinks of them, his tears might
stop. *Helen couldn't even write her name when I first met her. . . .
How did I do it all these years? She is still a dish, your mother, what
a behind she's got on her. She was pretty as all get out. What was she
doing marrying a kook like me?*

Her father wondered about death. He told her. And he wanted them to know—Helen and Lilly—that for all the selfishness in him, his state now was something he could not control. *My brother, Leon, a Republican, always said I wouldn't amount to anything. You remember him at the hospital, Lilly? Leon didn't give a damn. I wish him luck and he'll need it. . . .*

By the time the train pulled into Valhalla, three stops from Mount Kisco, the teenage girls were dozing off, and in her mind Lilly was going through what she would do once the train arrived in Mount Kisco, her own stop. Lilly watched the town of Mount Kisco appear slowly from the shortening distance. A rusted old fence was around the ghetto houses up on a hill past the train tracks, and the clapboard houses looked splintered and fenced-in as if an explosion had taken place, molding a dark cavity of poverty and peeling shingles and isolation. The tree branches stretched cadaverous into the lit sky where the shanty houses of the poorer Westchester stood.

The train halted at the Mount Kisco depot, and Lilly disembarked into the bright Westchester sunlight. She signaled for one of the taxis, and then she was a passenger again, on her way to her parents' house in Bedford.

The taxi passed the familiar century-old estates, the gargoyles and birdbaths, the lawns of affluent Bedford as Lilly's feelings ran amorphous over the acres of ravines and creeks. But the air was savory again as she remembered it, the pungent maple of the wooded expanses filling her. Someplace Lilly heard dogs barking.

Time had gone by so rapidly. Her father awoke from his coma in 1971. In the town of Bedford that summer, three years prior, families were collecting cans of pork and beans and powdered milk for the planes flying into Biafra. The magazines at the beauty salons and town country clubs were a couple of years old and filled instead with the story of Mary Jo Kopechne drowning at Chappaquiddick with Ted Kennedy, and with Woodstock. Images of Mary Jo Kopechne swam inside Lilly's head now—the photographs of the well-dressed senator leaving the scene of the accident.

Lilly always wondered how she would remember Bedford when she was older. The grass that was like delicate watercress. The trees—fragile, precious. Sugar maple trees, white birch and ash, evergreens and weeping willows, nature that was slender and sweet. The town's enclave of old colonial-type shops housed fragile china frogs and hand-blown glass paraphernalia, golden urns and even crucifixes from earlier times. There were still an old mill farmers' library and the Village movie theater, which played a Rock Hudson and Doris Day movie called *That Touch of Mink* when Lilly was thirteen. But in the 1600s, renegades, sorcerers, and witches were said to populate the area.

By noon, the taxi had pulled up to the Weills' sprawling white house, and it looked deserted. The taxi stopped by the path steps to the front door and let her out. Lilly felt the beginning of the long afternoon ahead like a weight larger than she thought she could endure.

The stone walkway was overgrown now with weeds, ugly stalks of green where ants crawled and circled, as if confused. There were no flower cups at the top of the stems anymore. Beyond a distant stone wall Lilly could still see the forest she used to walk in with her close friends from the high school: the nature in the near distance had remained clean—far enough away from the peeling paint of the house (which blew off in the winds and landed in shreds and clumps on the porch and grass), the unkempt rock gardens growing wild and crude.

As David and Lilly sat opposite each other at the dining room table that afternoon, they drank hot cocoa Lilly made for them in the kitchen. The afternoon light was jittery on her father's diminished gray hair, giving it almost a halo, a celestial absolution. As he talked on monotonously, making little sense, rambling, Lilly turned to watch the branches of her favorite white birch tree with its shredding bark wave in the wind outside the bow window.

The table was set, as if it were before. Old polished silverware, dabs of pink copper stain remover still on the knife and spoon handles, the forks' prongs. It was the day the housekeeper came. Lilly heard shuffling and sneezing, the off-and-on of the vacuum cleaner from the living room.

"What's the point?" David had asked her suddenly, looking up from his cup of cocoa. "Your mother left the house again. She works in that travel agency. She will go away again. Tell me if I was a good father."

"You were a good father, Daddy," Lilly had said.

"Your mother hates me. She sleeps in our old bedroom alone with that Sony television. The little one, I mean that looks like a box. Is it a television? Or does your mother just tell me that to get rid of me? She watches it so she doesn't have to listen to me anymore."

"No, Daddy. She just gets tired. She always liked to watch television."

"I want to buy tickets to get out of here," her father said, and then he started crying.

"Tickets?" she had asked him, finally standing to go over and quiet him. His face was a pale map of flaccid veins, his skin so thinned she could see his veins as tributaries crisscrossing on his cheeks and forehead—on his long nose, under the unshaven gray bristles on his upper lip, his chin.

The basement door had been closed for months now, and the snow gathered on the basement's outside door, freezing the bolts so that it could not be lifted from the outside anymore. Lilly had wondered if the frost had so damaged and rusted the door's hinges, it was sealed forever.

The maid left by 2 p.m. Lilly and David were still at the dining room table talking.

"Where's your mother? She needs to come and help me," David went on. "Tell your mother I am a broken man. Let me tell you a story of a man who lost his whole life—"The suffering on David's face was constant, pulling at him in abrupt shifts of intensity.

Lilly took his fingers under her right hand on the table and felt how cold they were, as if they were back in the hospital bed, three years before.

"I have only survived through my family love," he had said, but his expression was hollow, as if he were reading Hallmark cards. "Yes, my family has rescued me. I was a broken man," he started to cry again. Then Lilly saw that the cup of cocoa had scorched a corner on his thin lips, which began now to redden and then grow swollen.

"Daddy, what happened to your mouth?" Lilly asked him, alarmed.

"What?" he asked.

"To your mouth," she said. "What happened. Is the cocoa too hot? Daddy?"

"It's your mother," he said, bowing his head. "She makes me cry. We used to date and now she wants nothing to do with me."

"You mean Mom?"

"Yes, I think she went away."

"No, no, Daddy. She'll be back tonight. She's at work."

"What kind of man would let his wife work? You see what I mean?" He pushed his cup of cocoa away, making unnatural, strident heaves from his chest. "I'm so confused," he said. "Will I be better?"

He had made Lilly feel important. Sometimes David had given Lilly something she never felt. It could have been that he was now "dating" her, she had thought, almost laughing out loud that day at the strangeness of his loosened feelings.

"Let's see," he had continued, after long minutes at the table passed. "I think you're the one who understands me. We suffer in the same ways." When he talked like this, the room seemed to warm, the drifts of snow at the window looked startlingly like white gold. "I'm sick, aren't I?" he asked her again. "But love has saved me." Then he began another monologue, stiffly mumbling through his lips.

"Your mother always resented my intellect. She was an ignorant woman, and an hysteric," he explained to Lilly. "I'm a destroyed man. With only the love of my family to keep me going." Had he been a good father? He pleaded with Lilly, "Please tell me that I was a good father." Lilly believed she would suffocate listening to him again. Helen hated him because she resented and misunderstood him, he went on, continuing, "Your mother was so bitter, she even wanted to go back to Israel. Your mother is a very ill woman." Helen needed help since the day he married her, and he had once tried to find Helen a good psychiatrist in Westport but she wouldn't go. Did Lilly know that?

Later, Lilly helped him with his walker, taking him into the mudroom through the kitchen. Where he had fallen the night of his accident was now a bare, bloodless spot, smelling of Lestoil. She made him a light supper: a glass of orange juice and a sandwich of Brie cheese on rye bread with mustard and tomatoes. She left them and some Pepperidge Farm cookies on his tray in front of the old television with rabbit-ears antennas in the mudroom with him. She helped him adjust all the static on the TV, and then the six o'clock news came on. They watched an accident scene in Brooklyn live on *The Channel Two Evening Report*. Then Lilly went upstairs. Her father had tired of talking so much again.

She was returning to the scene of a crime she had committed as if in her sleep three years before, Lilly told herself, kneeling by the old bathtub that since had been scrubbed so raw, it looked like it was made of a rough white stone. She ran the tub water and listened to the hissing and creaks in the old water pipes, thinking this water had seduced her once. She was sure the tub had not been filled since that evening three years ago. There wasn't even a bar of soap on the rim, and Lilly wanted to cry uncontrollably, staring into the tub's deep space, which seemed vast as death.

Inside her parents' bedroom, a green valise was still filled with the gifts for family in Israel that Helen had bought before David's accident. Helen never fully unpacked it since the night of David's accident.

₪

Helen finally came home by 8 p.m. Lilly was already in her old childhood bedroom, undressed for bed. Her mother took her dinner upstairs where she could watch her Sony TV. Lilly heard her in the hall.

"Lilly, are you here?" Helen had called, and Lilly leaned out from behind the door for a brief moment to assure her mother she was there.

David wandered into Lilly's bedroom an hour later. And Lilly looked at him thinking, *Why am I a trash bin?* They could throw anything into her. She could be emptied. She could be filled. She could be carried from here to there with nothing but their waste. She didn't know whether her father had urinated in his pajamas before he came into her bedroom that night. Helen had buried herself by then down the hall in reruns of *The Perry Mason Show*; its theme music blared like a foghorn. The sticky but wet secretion from David's penis had flooded his pajama's crotch even before he sat on her bed. *It could have come from his nose*, Lilly had thought, or other orifices. The stain she suddenly noticed must have been there before he came into her room and not while he was with her because it was crusted, half-dry.

The moon came in through the oval window of her bedroom, and she had remained still, feeling the moonlight reflecting off the window glass and shingles of the house, as she could not keep her eyes off the blot in the place where her father's organ was cloaked under cloth and darkness. He continued to sit on the edge of her bed, talking to her, unaware. He did not touch her, and she knew that his discharge was not from arousal by her, as it had been there before he came into her room. He talked as if she wasn't really there.

David left her bedroom by midnight, but the image of his secretion had remained with Lilly. Lilly urgently started searching through her old dresser drawer for some paper to write on. She rifled through the loose socks and nightgowns still left in there from other times she slept over, but she found nothing to write on. It brought her to tears, when rummaging through useless knickknacks she had packed into old shoeboxes in the closet, that she still could not find any paper, pencil, or pen. The desperation became a burn inside her stomach. How could she forget to bring her notebook with her, she asked herself. Why did she forget?

"He doesn't realize what he is doing." It was Helen's old, firm self returning when her mother burst inside the bedroom door, the TV in her arms. "He molested you."

Lilly had heard him in her mother's bedroom. Helen must have seen David's pajama crotch stain before he went back downstairs to the mudroom. The TV had shut off, and they were arguing.

"Mom, no, that isn't true," Lilly protested. "He was not molesting me."

"I don't believe you," Helen said.

Lilly felt as if she had been pierced. "Mom—"

"No, no darling, I am not talking about me blaming you. Shah! I'm going to sleep with you now here! I must save you, I will protect you from him. We will watch the TV and go to sleep together now," Helen finished, bringing the tiny TV into her bed, clutching it, its cord dangling on Lilly's bedroom floor where Helen had moved a bureau to plug it into a wall outlet.

Helen slid under the wool blanket with Lilly, balancing the TV on her belly, and turning it on so that soft voices could be heard inside it, from an old movie or show. Lilly didn't look. Her mother's legs were so warm against Lilly's cold thighs. They could hear David below them by then, under the floorboards.

Why did her mother still smell so good? Lilly had wondered. It made Lilly angry, the fragrance of Helen's love. A vaginal scent got loose, too, with Helen's sweat; it grew, embracing and gratifying. Lilly remembered Helen's hands in the basement, over her bookbinding tools in the afternoons when everything around them seemed to be soft and dozy. Or, in the living room, the laughter of her mother in her summer dresses, laughing and drinking iced tea with half a lemon floating in the glass in the living room—the watercolor painting of Jerusalem behind her on the wall. The warm love from her mother swelled in Lilly's memory, a mixed blur—Helen taking her for St. Peter fish fillets at a seaside restaurant in Haifa the few times her mother took her to Israel as a young child, her loud breathing in a bed on the other side of a hotel room back then, too, near shutters, over the ancient streets. Lilly could somehow remember such details, but they were disjoined from any continuum of experience, just pieces of memory loose in her head. She could not place them in time.

There was something awful about her mother's warmth now. Something when they were lying together now made Lilly's heart beat too fast, a feeling too heavy, like a torrent, or like a violent blaze in her bowels. She wished she could feel the way it had been when she was young with her mother.

"What are you thinking about, darling?" Helen asked Lilly after a while. The television perched on her mother's stomach above the blanket began to play the late-night news. "Did your father touch you? Did he?"

"He didn't touch me at all, Mom."

"Did he hurt you, your father?" Helen asked Lilly. "The doctor told me; this is from the brain damage."

"No."

"He is someone else now, not your father, you must remember this. This bad man is not really who he was. He doesn't know what he's doing." Helen stroked Lilly's mussed hair and Lilly lay under her mother's soft touch, which soon brought Lilly to the center of absolute inertia. Both of them resided now in a permanent hardship, Lilly had thought, like an eternal winter. Helen eventually picked the TV off her stomach, and Helen's right arm spanned across Lilly's shoulder blade as Lilly turned on one side under the wool blanket, the hiss of the cruel March cold at the window. "Poor darling," Helen kept saying. "My poor, poor little Lillian."

A yellow light came through the window by 3 a.m. It cast a dry, pasty sheen on them both, Helen and Lilly, as if the eye of the moon had a cataract.

The strange light cut across the darkness.

After a while, it was as if Lilly hadn't been with her father at all. When Lilly awoke in the morning, she could see the ice and glinting slivers on the branches of the outside trees, on the window ledge and frame, but it felt watery and warm inside, as if they were floating in a strange lake all night inside a tower.

Chapter Six

In her hospital room now, Lilly stopped her thoughts from pulling at her. Voices inside her were telling her that being there in the house for her parents, a part of their sorrow, had been her own catastrophe.

She drew out a fresh pair of panties from the paper-lined drawer of the bureau she had just filled with the clothes Jane had brought her—a nice, clean cotton pair, which smelled like their apartment in Little Italy. Jane even went to the all-night Laundromat on Mott Street for her after leaving the emergency room, Lilly realized. Sat among the Italian single men with their slices of Genoa salami, white cheese, and flasks of bourbon, as the washing machines spun into the night. Lilly envisioned the Laundromat now again, set amid the Italian bread bakeries and an old, run-down medical clinic where a sign read, "Health Clinic for Bad Spines and Feet." The neighborhood mothers would be there by early morning in their hairnets and slippers, wearing winter coats, and doing their chores, transistors playing Frank Sinatra ballads from some radio station in New Jersey. They washed and folded for their large families as if by inner nature. The floor of the Laundromat was mopped glistening clean after the men left in the dawn, garbage emptied into the street cans, a morning of busy cleanups and mending, where the doings of Little Italy's private male circles in their secret meetings and the Bowery's wandering homeless plagued the neighborhood, littering its blocks of family tenements. When the women appeared on the block in the evening twilight, their bracelets looked like Egyptian amulets, black eyeliner with silver studs streaked their eyelids, and their breasts were big as tires. How different it was than the house of Lilly's parents, she thought now.

The taillights from cars in the hospital parking lot were flashing in a distance out the window now, and Lilly wondered what the mornings would be like in the hospital—if she would dream differently here, under the clean white sheets.

She remembered how slowly the morning sun rose in Little Italy, shaking out light over Elizabeth Street. Lilly was dreaming horrible dreams these weeks. The basement with her mother's bookbinding table was a prison in one of her dreams, a place of barred doors and windows, her mother's bookbinding tools implements of cruelty. And when she awoke, frightened and shaken, to the empty darkness of her Little Italy bedroom, the morning sky was so vast and cloudless she thought it would take hours for the sun to light it. The April wind was sweeping bits of Bowery refuse around the street.

All late winter the television sets were blaring from inside the Italian Florentine tenements. The news was all about Patty Hearst in February, the kidnapped nineteen-year-old daughter of the millionaire William Randolph Hearst Jr., a sylph of a girl. The kidnappers asked whether could they use the phone when they first burst into her apartment. Forced to the floor, Patty was gagged while her fiancé was beaten with a wine bottle. In the pictures of her fiancé, his tufts of brown hair and fair skin were like Mitchell's. The leader of the Symbionese Liberation Army stood over Patty. Maybe Patty had felt him the way Lilly felt Dr. Burkert in the seclusion room tonight, entering through her terrified pores. Then kidnappers started firing machine guns, and Patty was blindfolded, put into the trunk of a car outside the Berkeley apartment, and whisked away. Lilly remembered watching the activity on the streets from her balcony in Little Italy. The asphalt-scented wind became stronger once the sun rose, tickling the wet garments the Italian mothers pinned on their clotheslines in the dawn. The garments they abandoned to watch the details of the Patty Hearst story flew like flags of feminine armies high above the littered streets. Three or four TVs were blaring the news about the kidnapped girl by 10 a.m. that morning. The Italian mothers were at their kitchen tables early for their group coffee break. Lilly could hear them:

"She's just a girl."

"They want money."

"Nah, she's going to get herself raped."

"What're ya talking?

The men were out in the streets, still drunk from the night before, walking in pairs, returning from their haunts. The storefronts in Little Italy were draped in dull green curtains, the secret recesses between them filled with cigarette smoke rank with gin, floating out of forbidden windows. Lilly had watched the polyester-trousered men move to their shiny parked Cadillacs, shaking out their legs, pinching up the creases on their department-store pants, their physiques bulky as the bloody beef and pork carcasses hanging in the butcher shops off Houston Street. They were gathering for their usual morning conferences inside their closed cars while the sun sparkled from the cars' windows. Sometimes Lilly heard gunshots in the dank morning air, the noises muted and sounding like soda bottle tops popping off. There was a small gun shop on Mulberry Street. But that morning, the air was silent, except for the voices of those men.

All of it was so far away now, like Mitchell. *But hadn't Patty Hearst escaped her other life?* Lilly wondered now. *Maybe Patty found herself alone, too, in a sequestered room like this.* William

Randolph Hearst had held his press conferences on his front lawn a few hours later, and then the NBC special report played a tape of Patty's voice: "Mom, Dad—I'm okay. I had a few scrapes and stuff, but they've washed them up, and they're getting okay. I think it was just a way of confirming that I was alive." Lilly thought she sounded strangely happy, as if she had been abducted into a state of inexpressible bliss.

Lilly went to the window to look at the night expanding outside her room now. She didn't know whether she could change her life by being here. She peered down, into the gray cobblestones of the formal hospital walkway. She was five stories high.

Below the barred window, the moon lit a garden of lush, high-stemmed tulips—red as a woman's lipstick—festooned like elaborate embroidery around the trim building. Lilly could see all the way to the parking lot where the attendants held their stations, directing guests and visitors, their green jumpsuits well kept as the neo-Gothic hospital. She watched a taxicab pull up, and one of its doors opened; a well-dressed woman extended some shining bills to a driver. Suddenly the world outside felt threatening to Lilly again. The moonlight was an enemy light to her, illuminating the difference between the confident woman and Lilly. The dollar bills looked important as tickets back to a life that Lilly may never possess again.

Lilly lay down on the flossy mattress, exhausted. Again she felt too fragile. She was barely awake enough to feel the new dream moving under her thoughts. First, it felt pure and warm, in which she was young and pressed onto a nurturing mother's lap, a weight of no more than a butterfly. But a piece of the fantasy flickered in her imagination, and she made out the lips and cheekbones of the nurse Beverly gazing down at her.

Then it suddenly shifted, and Lilly was gagged and bound on a cellar floor, as if for punishment from a tall man who looked like the leader of the Symbionese Liberation Army. She was filling with anguish but it mixed with desire. Her body was shot into a terrible darkness, orgasming. Her hands tried to break loose from her bondage, to go to Beverly, yearning for the nurse's protection, for Beverly's lap, which appeared large and soft as a rescuing beach from a wild storm. But as the nurse drew close and Lilly felt Beverly against her, the same warm sexual drumming began again inside Lilly's flesh. Terror rippled through her, and Lilly lurched, panicked, from the bed.

Outside her hospital door she heard someone playing a country station. *Patsy Cline*, she thought, or someone like that. For a few moments, the woman's voice calmed her. The rest of the hall was quiet, as if shut down for the night.

But then Lilly had to stand by the window where even the radio sound couldn't reach her. She peered down at the parking lot again. The woman and the taxi were gone. Lilly watched the cloak of night lay over the grassy bank separating the hospital parking lot and its grounds. Trying to calm herself further from the dream, she gazed for a long time out the window.

She was glad Mitchell and everyone were gone, she thought. Hadn't she really wanted it this way? she asked herself.

The room was cooling. Lilly felt her overwhelming tiredness again. She unwrapped the two graham crackers she had taken from the snack tray in the lounge, laying them on top of her bureau. Her mouth was moistening. Her appetite was returning. She could trace the skeletal edges of her self-neglect with her fingers roaming under her hipbones, all over the thinner corners of her entire person.

It will be better now, she thought, finishing the graham crackers.

She took one hand and touched the top of her head, which seemed too hot an hour ago, as if some fever had begun. But even her hair felt cooler. And she went to turn off the lamplight over her tiny desk.

A few days ago, Lilly thought, she wasn't in this room. She had stood instead at the window of her flat in Little Italy and looked down on the streets. She had seen a shadow from a balcony next door, and the glass front from the delicatessen below glowed yellow as gold. The floor of her apartment bedroom was littered, too, and it could have been a street. She had yearned to join the shadows in their alternate world. To lie with them, behind a veil of life. *Death seemed so beautiful*, she had thought, like the feathers on the antique hats inside the stores on West Broadway.

Chapter Seven

The next morning, the light coming into Lilly's hospital room was a thick, warm arrow.

"This is Lilly Weill," Lilly heard a nurse say to somebody out in the hall, and then Lilly saw that her bedroom door was wide open to the same source of light spreading and scrolling off the hall tables, the bone walls.

"Could you please come with me?" A lab technician, wearing a salmon-colored uniform and holding a tray of carefully lined-up glass test tubes, was leaning into the room. "I'm here to draw bloods this morning," she said to Lilly. "Heard about you coming in this Monday night, so I guess you don't know the routine yet. Just put a robe on, then you can follow me down to the exam room. It won't take long, don't worry."

The woman was smiling at her, and Lilly run a hand through her hair, pulling down on its tangles and knots. Her hair seemed to have grown almost an inch in the few days she had been in the hospital.

Lilly slipped a thin bathrobe on over her nightshirt. She tried to swallow away her morning breath. Then, stepping into paper slippers, she followed the technician down the hall.

Lilly joined the seated line of patients waiting to have their blood drawn. She tried not to feel like a captive in this sullen world of weird people and rules. When, after a few minutes of waiting in her armchair, the line to the examination room thinned—patients walking out, pressing cotton swabs to the inside of their elbow—Lilly suddenly worried that Helen might have called in the night and demanded to them that Lilly must come home now. This was why she was getting a blood test—because they were under orders to discharge her today.

The technician called Lilly's name, smiling at her again, and holding open for her the door to the examination room.

The metal exam table under the squares of unlit fluorescent light brought back—for a moment—her falling apart that first night of admission. But now in the morning sunlight the room seemed very different; it was as ordinary as a family doctor's consulting room. No ominous instruments or probing lights were loaded on the cabinet table, and Lilly wondered whether she had imagined them that night. *It could have been part of a dream*, she told herself, but then she felt a dull throb in her groin and suddenly thought she recognized a small flashlight and metal speculum.

"You looked frightened," the technician was saying. "It's just routine for every patient here." The technician pulled up one sleeve of Lilly's bathrobe. Lilly's mind glided into an easy blankness, feeling the technician's fingers patting down a vein inside her right arm as Lilly tried to stay perfectly calm, gazing up at the cool-white tiles of the ceiling, as if she were treading water.

₪

That morning when they were drawing bloods, Lilly had been a patient in the hospital for one whole night and morning. The spring rose like a deep green haze inside the ward. From the sky outside the hospital's windows, warm winds periodically blew in when an attendant allowed a window to be jarred open.

For the next, beginning days, Lilly worked herself through the group of milling patients regularly, accepting their sympathy, answering questions about who she was again.

Lilly quietly watched the other patients as she sat in a lounge chair, silent but observant, waiting for the chiming bells that signaled meals and community meetings. She studied her own dislocation through their reflecting faces and movements.

The electronic chimes also rang from amplifiers inside the nursing stations at 7 a.m. every morning on the ward, rousing the patients for compulsory showers and then breakfast. Through the windows the sun—just rising—seemed to exhale breaths of light all across the green hall carpet.

Observing the other patients, Lilly put them into two categories: those who seemed like mourners on a long stretch of night, lost in their memories, and those who looked like they were enjoying a vacation from outside influences, stretching themselves noisily into limitless freedoms of thoughts and feelings, vocal and un-self-consciously unhinged.

The news of the kidnapped Patty Hearst—who had by April transformed into a bank robber for the Symbionese army—was in all the newspapers lying around the ward, broadcasted on the morning and evening news as if an unhealthy obsession had taken over the outside world as Lilly and the other mental patients were tucked away, inside the hospital. On the six o'clock news, they again played the tape of Patty Hearst speaking to her parents from a tape recording made in the house of the Symbionese Liberation Army. Mr. Hearst's appearance in front of microphones on his lawn—explaining to the press he did not know who or what group had taken his daughter, but he was sure she was being forced to rob banks for them—was replayed over and over again, like a trailer for a lurid action movie.

One dawn, Lilly woke hearing voices outside her door. The sunlight was warming her room early. Though the air was still stuffy, it contained the faint scents of the lilac and spruce trees outside in the grassy dirt beds.

"For he's a jolly good fellow—" A male voice was singing outside the door.

"Which nobody can deny—"

"Which nobody can deny—"

Lilly put her robe on. It was early, but breakfast might have started and she may have slept through the chimes. She didn't keep track of time with a clock in her room. She ventured out into the hall, barefoot and tentative.

Leonard, in blue pajamas, was seated in the huge armchair by the hall table, which held an empty vase. He had swung one of his big legs over the arm of the chair. There was a graham cracker cake on his lap he hadn't touched, frosted with what looked like Hershey's syrup. He seemed to be humoring those around him. There was another male patient eating graham crackers from a cardboard box, cross-legged on the carpet runner. He stared up at Leonard admiringly as a third man continued to sing.

"Which nobody can deny—which nobody can deny—," the third man droned on.

"Do another song," the seated patient suddenly exclaimed. "That one really sucks."

A nurse poked her head from the nurses' station. "Keep your voices down. Patients are still in bed," she said.

"It's the man's frigging birthday," the singer said.

"Happy birthday, Leonard," the nurse said as she came abruptly out from the station. "How about singing real softly? Celebrate, but do it really softly."

"It's the man's birthday."

"There are people sleeping," the nurse said. "This isn't your living room."

Lilly felt the steady, firm gaze of Leonard's eyes on her face. He looked calm and unfazed, even as the nurse continued to direct the group on how to celebrate his birthday. A beard had started on his chin that was thick and sparkled with reddish strands. His pajama shirt was open, and she could see the fullness of the same strands on his chest, oddly soft and long. He smelled of something basic and masculine; it could have been a smoky peat. He seemed impervious to the infantilizing situation in which Lilly found herself. His imperturbability fascinated and shook her. She was barefoot, she suddenly remembered, feeling naked. And she was in her nightgown, a thin, insubstantial robe. What was she thinking coming out here? She started to tremble.

"You need to take better care," Leonard said, half-chastising her as he ignored the nurse. "This is all just stupid stuff. They wanted to celebrate in the middle of the night." He placed the paper plate on the carpet, and she realized she was glad he hadn't touched it. There was nothing childish about the man who was talking to her now, and for the time being she wouldn't have to feel let down and opened to the belittling nurse. Leonard's largeness and his intense, curious face allowed her feelings to grow increasingly warmer toward him. Lilly lost track of where the nurse and the two other patients were.

"Please don't worry. I'm sorry if we woke you." The lamplight seemed to climb up his neck, to make his face the center of the brightness. She expected to feel that awful state—as when she thought she was becoming part of other people—but she felt, instead, as if she were re-forming into the person Leonard was examining now so intensely with his gray eyes. Her body was present.

"Don't worry," he said to her. "They won't keep you here a long time. I can tell you're someone they won't keep in this hospital."

"I didn't mean to come here at all," she said. "I hope they'll let me out soon."

"I hope so, too."

"Thank you," she said. And then she quickly turned from him, still feeling him watch her. His gaze pressed into her as she went back into her private room, and whether from his stare or her attraction, she was relieved she didn't have to talk to him anymore.

She found herself in front of the mirror in her room, glimpsing at herself as if parts of her were suddenly coming back.

₪

The ward began to captivate Lilly—strangers and safety. The locked doors were protecting her, she thought, and she was all right amid the other captives. As the days progressed, the faces in the lounges felt soft-eyed when they gazed at Lilly as she entered during the afternoons, after lunch. Patient tears and shouting were common on the ward, a part of its language, as frequent as "Hello, how are you?" Each night, a cat-footed nurse on the night shift opened the door and threw Lilly a "Hello," and Lilly had heard an unnamed patient screaming, "Mama, help!" for three consecutive nights, somewhere down the dark corridor.

Finally, Lilly felt a physical tension overwhelm her when the nurse checked her in bed the third night. Lilly froze, not answering her.

The next day Lilly watched the TV with Lisa and a few other patients until the calm was temporarily broken in the afternoon around 3 p.m. when, with a raw howl and squealing, Spia took down her panties, plopped into the baskets of trash, and defecated, producing steaming rolls of shit and smells that debased the tranquil air.

Spia hollered, "Bingo!" in the middle of the south corridor. "Watch me dance, you motha-fuckas." The tawny-skinned woman had lifted up her arms over her head. *She was strong-willed and loose, like Helen*, Lilly thought. Then suddenly Spia was naked, her pubis sparking in the hall light, its hairs a black curly weave. Spia had tightened her already taut buttocks cheeks, and began rotating her hips and belly dancing. "I'm Cleopatra, ain't I, girl?" she cried out, and rolled her hips until her arms dropped down and then she sunk to her knees and started masturbating. Then her index finger thrust itself into the cave beyond her vaginal lips, into her black velvet womb. "Hey, I'm crazy," she hollered at no one in particular. "Yes, ma'am. I'm crazy, and I'm queen of the Nile!"

The staff sailed a bedsheet out to cover Spia. It took four male aides, two nurses, and Caroline to harness Spia under the sheet and drag her to the quiet room. They cleaned up her mess in the garbage pails.

The next afternoon, Spia again excreted unspeakable piles of waste products from her rearing body all over the hall. And the hall stank ferociously with the sewage of her revenge again.

Spia would explode into vicious rage each time they took her up from her squat and carried her back into the quiet room, an incontinent and enormous child—usually four nurses, one on each arm, one on each kicking leg, Spia swinging between them. Each time Spia was let out in the late evening after dinner, she stayed in the lounge watching TV with the others, messy and groggy, but compliant. Then by the next afternoon she was suddenly thundering again, galloping like a bucking horse, throwing all its riders off down the corridor.

As Lilly watched her frantic shadows on the corridor walls—the ward became terrifying those times—she started watching herself, too. In one of her night dreams, Lilly was with her mother in a bath of warm water. They were in the baptistery, and someone was screaming for her mother like the unnamed patient down the corridor. But then Lilly and her mother were in the same bathtub as the night of her father's accident. Together they started swimming out into a sea, and Lilly felt comforted before the terror of being helplessly submerged awakened her.

Some of the other patients seemed to disappear after they threw public fits and seizures. But there was no suggestion that Spia would be sent away. Spia continued on the ward with hardly a sign that the staff had altered her scheduled defiance against them.

₪

In the center lounge one afternoon toward the end of Lilly's first week in the hospital, the patient named Cecilia, a hairdresser from Queens, was speaking in rapid Spanish and English, gesticulating wildly with her hands as she began describing the beating her husband had given her one night in her kitchen in Queens.

"He came at me, and my heart is beating. He hits me with his hands like I am a bag. I am hurt very bad, you see?" She lifted up her blouse to expose the marks on the small of her back. "Ay, yi yi," she said, "look here, and here, see?" Her bruised flesh was like a brown peach. "No escapes del Hombre de la Motosierra," she said. "You cannot escape the Chainsaw Man, did you see this movie? The killer looks just like my Jorges in this pelicula."

"Oh, Cecilia," Wendy exclaimed. "Poor Cecilia." Wendy's eyes were reddening, as if drugged.

Lilly, watching them, began to feel dizzy, imagining this story of Cecilia's beating in her mind—the husband, Jorges, cornering Cecilia in her kitchen against a steaming pot of dinner casserole. Pounding her flesh into submission, tearing off her clothes—Cecilia defenseless, and he possessing a divine strength because now Cecilia was crying out, "Mi Dios! Mi Dios!" groaning and gasping, but transfixed.

Lilly, pitched inside the center of this brutality, felt flushed, as if drowning in the images rushing through her head. A building excitement inside Lilly turned into a burn, and then, as Cecilia kept talking, Lilly felt a relentless desire to pee—a reflex that might relieve the indiscriminating throbbing in her lower abdomen.

"Please stop, it will be all right." Wendy was trying to calm Cecilia's passionate display of body and sounds.

"If I fall asleep he'll get me in my dreams," Cecilia was saying.

"He can't get in the ward," Wendy urgently told Cecilia.

At last, unable to contain herself, Lilly fled from the lounge and its voices. She escaped down the corridor, into her private room. She closed its door and lay still on her bed until the excitement and tumult slowly left her body.

It was still afternoon when Lilly began composing her sign-out letter on hospital stationery, which stated simply, "Please discharge me after seventy-two hours. I have read the patient manual, and I am fully aware this will mean I am released against medical advice."

In the evening, Lilly handed in her sign-out letter, walking through the hall in her heavy Frye boots to make herself look and feel tough when she slipped the letter into the hands of the nurse in charge of the south station.

Later, alone in her room at the small desk, she spread out a notebook she bought from the mobile canteen that rolled through the corridors every Wednesday, but she couldn't write. She still felt flooded by her feelings, as if a huge wave had taken her under it.

When the night fell, she undressed into her nightgown. She tried to think about packing her things in seventy-two hours; of when to call Jane to ask her to leave money downstairs for a taxi home; of how much she dreaded more outbursts from Cecilia, or maybe another patient.

But, unable to sleep, Lilly imagined herself on the train to Mount Kisco, going back to Helen and her father. And then she felt Helen enclosing her. They didn't need her father's brain damage to curl up inside one another, she remembered. They were doing it all along, weren't they? Long before David's accident. If Lilly left the hospital, Helen would get into her again and take over. How horrifying her mother was when she took over with her tyrannizing power. As if flames were leaping in her head, Lilly was seized by her mother's tyrannical power gripping her body, a huge roiling torrent. "Stay with me, Lilly, I am afraid of my life." Helen would tell her again.

It would destroy the bulb if she went back to Helen and her father. The bulb would be obliterated, and then she would have to kill herself. Going home scared her more than staying in the hospital.

Lilly retracted her sign-out letter early the next morning.

₪

Dr. Burkert entered her room after breakfast that same morning. His face was boyish, but his voice—low, steady—was mature, and reassuring in the same way the neo-Gothic locked doors gave off a subliminal signal of safety.

"Are you feeling calmer?" he asked her. His accent reminded her of the British-Palestinian intonation of her mother's voice. But nothing else was like her mother, she told herself, except this British intonation. He was not a man who had outbursts, she reassured herself, but he was powerful in his dominating remoteness, and it scared her. He was so thin. She made herself imagine his ribs under his shirt, and then his lack of bulk calmed her.

"I see you put in a sign-out letter," he said.

"I took it back," she said very quickly. She did not want to tell him about her dread of Helen taking over and how that kept her here. "There was a fight on the ward, not really a fight, and it frightened me. It was a mistake for me to write the sign-out letters and hand them in. I feel okay now."

By lunchtime, Lilly finally closeted her Frye boots—too heavy to wear on the ward—and she settled for the pair of hippie Tibetan slippers the patient, Louise, lent her. Louise kept feather boas, sun hats, assorted shawls, and costume jewelry—all in her private collection inside the closet in her room where Louise also set up a makeshift beauty salon. Patients could come and sit in Louise's room during the day and get their hair curled. In her bureau drawers, she harbored curling irons, combs, and other salon equipment that Louise received special permission to keep because her hairstyling and makeshift beauty shop were part of her therapy. Louise could do anything but cut hair because scissors were barred from patients' grasp. She was close to being discharged.

₪

In the following days, Lilly gradually felt herself as part of the corridors—the winding green canvas carpet connecting the south side and north side, the clean bricks of the large hospital building, and the lounges where circles of smoke were illuminated by the sunbeams from the windows. And Lilly was able to keep herself from the way things were before her admission. She found refuge when she felt she was more in control, eating her suppers (lamb chops or cube steak or Hawaiian chicken supreme), glad to be there among the secure promise of solid meals, of a full milk carton on the trolley offered by the kitchen staff with yellow cake and chocolate frosting, the hum of the April air conditioning.

Weekday mornings, the patients went up to a gym on the top floor. The ward was almost empty.

Lilly returned to her usual spot on the green couch in the lounge. The feel of a warmer breeze reminded Lilly of the encroaching summer, of time crawling closer toward her.

She was still excused from recreational and occupational therapy on the eighth floor where most of the patients were. On the green couch, she could kneel and see the FDR Drive out the lounge window and watch the new cable car taking passengers to Roosevelt Island. She rested here every morning after an early breakfast, and later, after lunch—her notebook resting under her arm in the hope she would be able to write again, watching the workmen do more work on the cable car.

The cable car to Roosevelt Island was on a long wire strewn far into the sky over the river. It looked like a ski lift and brought the people from the Manhattan side to the brand-new glistening buildings on Roosevelt Island. They arrived in the morning with tin lunch boxes and helmets. Soon their boots were crusted with muck. She watched them examining the cars, inspecting them, ensuring that the cars did not fall but passed smoothly over the dirty water with its fierce currents. *They must be reliable people*, Lilly thought to herself, *building the cars for travelers to reach such a new place.*

Did they ever see her? She had wondered, there on her knees, hands outstretched on the sill, watching them.

₪

As more days passed, Lilly's bulb continued to appear intermittently, unexpectedly, sometimes feeling like an intrusion, but there were hours when Lilly didn't feel its presence at all. If she had to think about it, she told herself, she could understand the bulb as a metaphor that was Lilly—her whole confusing existence, body, and soul. It enabled her to purchase a moratorium from life, college, other people, and the awful slavery of bodily magnetisms that made her blow and swell and respond helplessly, a leaf in a hurricane.

One night, Lilly was shivering cold, unblanketed in her bed as she tried to fall asleep. It was an unseasonably cold and nasty night. The air conditioners were left on all over the ward, and maintenance had not turned off their power.

Lilly twitched and shifted under her bedsheet. But by midnight, she had to get up. She had to ask the night nurse to get her a blanket.

The hall was lit only with table lamps that night. The nurse on call came out of the nurses' station carrying her clipboard and notes under her arm.

"Yes, it's freezing," the night nurse said to Lilly. "Let me go to the custodian's closet and get you a blanket."

The patient in the next room called out in agitation, "Can you please come!"

"I'll be a moment," the nurse said to Lilly, laying down her clipboard on a side table. A few minutes later, the nurse hurried out of the upset patient's room, and rubbing at her arms to warm her own body, she trotted off down the corridor to the custodian's closet.

The nursing notes on her clipboard were still on the hall table.

"April 17," Lilly read from her own file, stealing the clipboard and notes off the table. She needed to read very quickly before the nurse returned and caught her:

Patient was still somewhat agitated this evening,
though less so than when she was released from

the quiet room, two days ago, on the day of her admission (April 16).

April 19. Patient appeared calmer today, but does appear distracted at times. At these times, seems to become anxious, and withdrawn, possibly with body delusions. She spends much of her time writing in a notebook and reading. Some socializing in center lounge.

April 20. Patient was agitated this morning. Last night, patient turned in a sign-out letter but withdrew it within an hour. She wrote another sign-out letter this morning but again withdrew it. Patient became more agitated when morning nurse asked for her to report her feelings.

April 22. Admission symptoms of discomfort in pelvic area addressed by Dr. Burkert in staff meeting. Patient has a fear of intimacy, which causes her to become agitated and withdrawn. These fears seem related to her bodily symptoms, possibly with delusional content. No further physical examination seems necessary at this time as no abnormalities were found on her initial physical examination. However, the initial pelvic exam elicited extreme agitated response which lasted for some hours.

Anxiously, Lilly looked up now and peered down the corridor. *The night nurse must have been detained*, she thought. She continued to read faster, flipping through pages.

Patient presents as a young attractive twenty-year-old woman who appears anxious and

distracted. Can be avoidant of contact and intimacy which seem to precipitate her agitation.

Lilly saw the nurse, a gray blanket in her arms, coming
down the corridor. Lilly's eyes scanned the last page quickly
before the nurse could see her reading.

PRIMARY THERAPIST'S REPORT. DR. HOWARD
BURKERT, MD.   CHIEF COMPLAINT: Overdose
with 35x 5 mg, Librium tablet and half a bottle of
scotch.

PRESENT ILLNESS: Patient was admitted through
the emergency room on April 16 for an overdose.
She became uncooperative during the pelvic examination by a staff nurse. . . .

When the nurse finally arrived back, a blanket for Lilly
under her arm, she hadn't noticed the clipboard was moved.
She whisked the notes back, pushing the clipboard against her
bosom, telling Lilly she was sorry about the use of the air con-
ditioner during such a cold night.

₪

One afternoon, Lisa sat down on the couch next to Lilly,
and together they watched *The Little Rascals* and then reruns
like *Flipper*, *My Three Sons*, and *Gilligan's Island.* They went into
a trance—the cool, close air inside the lounge on their skin,
cold sweetness in their mouths from their soda and bananas.
Then Lisa became strident suddenly, red with discomfort for
no reason Lilly could understand. *This girl with freckled lips was
too volatile*, Lilly thought, and looked childish in her corduroy
jumper and ponytail, which reminded Lilly of awkward girls in
summer camp when Lilly was twelve.

"Did you see all the ovens up there in O.T.?" Lisa was de-manding. "I don't mean the kilns for those stupid ashtrays we have to make, but *ovens* to bake cakes from package mixes in that horrible new kitchen they built up there. We're treated—" She drove herself into a frenzy, her lips wetted by the words she spat out. "It's all so humiliating," she said, and then repeated, "The forces of humiliation are all around us."

Lisa suddenly fell quiet, and Lilly saw that Leonard had entered the lounge. He seemed calm and remote as he took a seat near them with his reading materials. Lilly felt his eyes gaze at her with unblinking attention. But she wasn't sure if he meant his look as inviting, or he was just trying to critically ap-praise her as the new face on the ward.

He seemed to completely take up the space that Lisa had occupied. She had heard from Lisa a few days before that he was getting his doctorate in physics, which had been inter-rupted by a sudden violent act he committed in the middle of Grand Central Station a few months prior. It was the hall's common knowledge that Leonard had a gun that afternoon, and that several innocent people had been lacerated by an ex-plosion he created, shattering an enormous glass and vinyl Ko-dak advertisement on the wall with two bullets. The reasons for his actions were mysterious, hidden behind his calm remote-ness. Leonard never grew impatient with the questions he was asked, but he wouldn't talk about himself or what happened in Grand Central Station. There was a darkness about him.

His face was pale, as though unused to sunlight, Lilly thought. Not exactly quiet as much as unavailable. His hard-cover texts on physics, anatomy, and philosophy were meticu-lously earmarked with different-colored strips of tape. There was a slight rip in his brown corduroy trousers, and one of his lean legs could be seen, through another tear over his knee-cap. He sometimes had a suit on for his court appearances, his tie loosened, its knot rebellious to the task, and he wore a pair of shiny brown oxford shoes. He seemed like a brooding hero out of a Shakespearean tragedy. *Like Hamlet*, Lilly thought, beginning to feel the bumpy pressure of his attractiveness, of his handsome, sharp shoulders and profile. He was careless in his hygiene, exuding the sweet but unwashed odors that drew her to him.

Leonard looked up at her on the couch. He raised one of his arms, and she could see he was sweating. The wet marks had turned his ordinary shirt a dark, police uniform blue.

Lisa, looking distressed, got up and left the lounge.

"It's really hot," Leonard said to Lilly after a few moments of silence.

"Yes," she said. He made her feel like a small girl. He was six feet four, Lilly calculated now, but despite his well-made looks, Leonard was held in like a celibate priest.

"A lot of it has to do with the building. The engineering system is old," he went on.

"Yes," she said again. "I imagine that's true."

He went back to his books, but in the next few minutes, he had looked up and smiled at her, and his gray eyes had looked deeper into her.

The lounge emptied slowly that evening. "Have you read Hobbes?" Leonard asked Lilly when they were finally alone. "The pathology of nature? What struck me is his belief in a state of anarchy. It fascinates me."

"Is that why you're here?"

"Partly. I'm here for a mind-body problem," he said.

"Oh."

"There's a primitive side to all of us. "

"You're right," she said, but only because she was very nervous.

"If you believe in free will, you can't understand physics. They are incompatible concepts."

"Why?"

"Because physics tells us there are laws beyond our control, no free will. Free will is an illusion."

Except for his dress, which looked messier than it might have been if he were on the outside, Leonard seemed to not belong there. The hospital and the ward seemed alien to his whole makeup, just the way it did to Lilly. Sitting near him seemed to bring back the smell of college rooms at Sarah Lawrence, of the library when it was dark outside, and a sweet pain came with remembering all that. She imagined him as a sharp, tall student in the Columbia University halls.

"Hobbes said that anarchy was the true nature of man," Leonard continued. "We are all by our natures a pathology, and without government of an absolute kind we will resort to our pathology. It's myself I fear." He paused. "My older brother Alex killed himself in the woods using a kitchen knife," he suddenly said now.

She startled. "I'm so sorry," she said.

He leaned toward her, but he really wasn't looking at her. It seemed a more tormented state that possessed him. "Maybe I should stay in the cage here. It is sort of like a cage we're in," he said. Then, after a long hesitation, Leonard added, "You should know I enjoy our discussions. I have to go back to the court tomorrow, but I enjoyed talking with you."

Leonard stood up, and Lilly saw again how tall he was. His large hands made her think of the men down below the lounge's window in the mornings, working on the cable car to Roosevelt Island, giving her a fragile hope.

₪

Alone in her bedroom, Lilly laid on her back on the bed-spread, pulling her light blanket over her, still dressed, the sheets untouched. Her hand moved under her jeans, and she let herself feel her skin as a fantasy was taking her. In her fantasy, Leonard pulled her across his clothed corduroy lap. She saw the rips over his knees and he was slapping her, but then he was arched above her in a sudden shift. His beating hand became a penis, send-ing her into a turbulence of pleasure. She was still warding off the sensations where the bulb lay, or she would travel bodiless through the air, she thought. A pressure in her was exciting her, and like a hand it met her in a passageway between her yearning and her resistance, pulling her into a place where blood began to circulate as mercury inside her. She didn't know which path to choose for a few moments, losing herself inside the pure cha-otic heat of her skin, of her body, breaking apart, giving into a storm within her, or the other—withdrawing, which would re-turn her into a state of psychotic inertia. But fear raised higher the fire inside Lilly; it was engulfing her. She came in a fierce orgasm, a sudden power in this wilderness of being. She awoke from the fantasy in sweat and trembling.

The image of him was dissipating as she regained reality. She felt awfully alone again.

₪

Leonard was gone from the hall the next morning, dressed to appear at his court trial downtown. Lilly saw him in the dis-tance after dinner; he was still in his suit and tie. He went into his room, but he didn't come out.

That night, a recurring dream began its appearances to Lilly. Its incarnations varied only slightly from night to night as the long days and evenings in the hospital progressed. The first night Lilly was a stowaway who must live with an adopted fam-ily. In the dream, all the adopted children are prisoners in their orphanage. Lilly is a skinny, unwanted girl. A brutally sculpted but beautiful man arrives. He is really an escaped convict who is very dangerous. He approaches her and is very attractive, in rough, worn blue jeans. There is anger all around in the orphanage—other prisoners screaming furiously. Lilly imagines herself abducted by him in the dream. The convict takes her by the wrist and pulls her across his knees. He spanks her and an orgasm is about to burst as his hand strikes light blows, thrilling her.

Then her well-dressed adopted sister who looks like Lisa, the patient, shows Lilly thick scars on her buttocks and back and tells Lilly the same convict had beaten Lisa almost to death. The convict who claims to be her lover will beat her almost to death, and Lilly becomes panicked, terrified. She cannot control her attraction to him, though she will be destroyed and the spanking-producing orgasms will become a fierce, homicidal beating.

The recurring dream paid its unwanted visits in her sleep, and the sudden snaps of orgasm woke and humiliated her. She couldn't control them.

After she jolted awake, she lay still in her bed. But a soreness was everywhere, as if she had been pulled to the floor, pummeled, her buttocks bruised and torn by imagined hands.

Lilly tried to stay awake all night, to not sleep and dream. Something invisible in the air was intoxicating and dangerous. She felt a trembling inside her head; an earthquake was down below. She couldn't tell what was inside her or what was outside.

It was as if parts of herself were swimming into one another.

Two days passed. Leonard left in the mornings for court, returning in time for dinner, and she could have moved toward him, but then she thought she might have imagined anything between them at all, that he had noticed her at all. He most likely thought she was pathetic, in her hospital pallor and her overly pleasing eagerness, she decided. She could have asked him about his hours in court and he would have been polite, she thought, but nothing more.

Chapter Eight

"Any mail today, Lilly?" Lisa asked, interrupting Louise. It was late afternoon, around 4:30, the start of Lilly's third week in the hospital. A soft rain was falling outside, and the afternoon outing to the Central Park zoo had been cancelled. The three women—Lilly, Lisa, and Louise—had been sitting for a long hour together. Louise was on the couch, next to Lilly. Lisa had settled into an armchair facing both of them. Leonard was always at court now, in the mornings until dinnertime, and Lilly was getting used to seeing his usual chair in the lounge empty.

Patty Hearst was on the front page of all the hall newspapers this week, too. Lilly was wondering again, staring into the newspaper pictures, about the puzzling transformation of the young Patty, whether her lanky, coffee-colored Symbionese lover in his cape and silver belt buckle of a seven-headed cobra was kind to her, if in the photos she was carrying the memory of his love. In the new photos, Patty was dressed as one of the Symbionese bank robbers with a loaded machine gun slung across her shoulder; her transformation showed her willowy, vulnerable form cloaked in a black Symbionese Liberation Army overcoat just like the other members of his gang, her fine hair tucked under an Afro wig.

"My gun was loaded. I am a soldier of the people's army now," Patty said into a tape recording for the public days later.

Something had happened to Patty in the labile moments between her fragmentation and self-re-creation, Lilly thought yesterday when she saw the pictures. She wondered if her kidnapper drew out Patty's pleasure, and Patty was hooked, brainwashed by orgasms.

The patients returned to the hall after activities. After lunch, the hall became a community of disparate groups, congregating in the lounges, their private rooms, the hall lounges.

Only one other patient, Frank, was in the lounge with the three women now. Frank was seated a distance away in an armchair studying the backgammon board he had laid out on a table, trying to think out his afternoon game with some of the other men.

"I was talking to Lilly," Louise said to Lisa now. "You're interrupting me, Lisa."

"Well, were you really saying anything, Louise?" Lisa asked. The track of scars on the inside of Lisa's left arm began to blaze up in the sunlight from the lounge window—a long, furrowed line seamed into her flesh. Lisa had opened her veins with a razor blade in her suicide attempt at her parents' home a few months ago, Lilly had learned eventually from other patients. Lisa never talked about it, and Lilly didn't ask her to. She had studied piano at Barnard before she was hospitalized, she was telling Lilly this morning, and now she had decided not to go back to the music department. Earlier, too, Lisa had given Lilly a manila folder marked "Alternative Files." Lisa had told Lilly that she would enjoy reading what was inside it. But Lilly hadn't opened it yet. Instead, she had set it aside on the windowsill when Louise started talking to her.

"Lisa, could you let me finish talking to Lilly, puh-leeze?" Louise said now. "I wanted to tell Lilly that she looks ravishing today."

Lilly blushed and blinked at Louise's words as if a flake of dust were tickling her eyelashes. "When you first came with those scary eyes, I thought you looked like Patty Hearst on a starvation diet," Louise said to her. "I love your eyes, honey."

"Thank you. I appreciate your comments," Lilly said to Louise stiffly. But she felt herself pulled in. Among them, it seemed, was a place like a station platform, where they all were held indefinitely, waiting in anticipation, in case one of them might suddenly understand something that would help the others move on. Sitting in this web of strange women this afternoon, Lilly wasn't thinking about the recurring spanking dream with the criminal who had become nameless, unidentifiable. By repetition, the dream had taken on a kind of grandeur. Maybe she should stay up tonight, Lilly was thinking now, watch the late news with Lisa, and keep avoiding sleep. She let herself sit in the lounge and talk with the women these days until the night nurse came to chase them all back to their rooms by midnight. She hoped the women would be there tonight again, too—when the recurring dream threatened. Lilly did not have to get too close to them or be afraid of them, as they didn't ask too much of her.

Louise was questioning Lilly now, "Are you all right, cupcake?"

"Yes," Lilly said. "I'm just thinking." She let go of a breath. There would be talk, and the television repairman came in this morning, she thought; the Magnavox had been on the blink for days, but now it was fixed.

"You think too much, Lilly," Louise went on. "You'd be a lot better if you didn't talk like a book."

"Lilly and I talk a lot," Lisa said to Louise.

"I never hear Lilly talk to anyone," Louise said.

"She comes alive at night," Lisa replied.

"I thought when you first came in you were just snotty because you talked like a book," Louise continued. "I'm not trying to say I don't like snotty people. Those people in their shell, I mean. But some of those college chicks make fun of me. The ones you probably hang out with. I'm not trying to judge you."

"I'm sorry, Louise," Lilly said. "I think you are mistaken. I don't hang around with people like that."

"Lilly doesn't look like Patty Hearst," Lisa interceded now. "Are you insane, Louise?" Lisa started flapping a *New York Times* she had whisked off the lounge table. "Patty Hearst loves fascists," Lisa muttered now. "Patty Hearst is sick."

"Do you know this for sure, Lisa?" Louise asked her.

"Yes," Lisa said. "The system is fascistic. And so is *he*."

"Who?" Louise asked.

"The criminal who kidnapped her. The Symbionese guy. Listen to this bullshit: 'Today, Patty Hearst read a tape-recorded plea to the public. She has joined the Symbionese Liberation Army,'" Lisa read from the newspaper. "She's holding a machine gun, for Chrissake."

"So, big deal," the patient named Frank suddenly exclaimed from his distant seat. "She's a dyke. She dresses up like a man. Then she thinks she's black, so she gets an Afro wig. What's the big deal? The woman is a cunt."

"No, she isn't. That isn't true, Frank," Louise said, angering.

Frank stood up from the backgammon table. "Yes, she is," he said. His belly was large, and his bathrobe was disheveled and unbuttoned, his large stomach spilling out like a huge bag of groceries stuffed behind his undershirt. "And anyway, I don't give a good goddamn about Patty Hearst. You ladies are too much for a man. A man needs his rest." He stared into the backgammon board and then tucked in his shirt.

The women looked up at him blankly as he stashed the cigarette pack he had put on the backgammon table into his pants pocket, preparing for one of them to respond to him.

"I'm feeling anxious," he said to them. "I need to talk to someone. I had a rough day yesterday. My wife came to visit. I need support. You know, to get things off my mind."

He moved closer to the women, his mouth opening, expecting he would tell them whatever it was that deserved their attention. But when none of the women responded to him still, he angrily turned and stormed away down the corridor.

"Patty Hearst showed them!" Louise shouted at his vanishing form, her eyes blazing. "Good for you, Patty! Now you're talking, Patty Hearst. Don't let people take their shit out on you! You exist, too, Patty Hearst!" Finished, Louise turned to Lisa and Lilly again and smiled, satisfied. "Patty screwed that Symbionese guy," she said. "Pardon my French."

"No, no, Louise," Lisa said now. "It wasn't like that. He locked her in a closet and used her body. It's so clear how he brainwashed her. She was taken away and exploited."

"I thought you said she was sick!"

"Sick people are always exploited, don't you know that? Because they feel like nothing."

"Maybe Patty Hearst just wanted to be a bank robber, Lisa," Louise said. "Maybe she wanted to be a soldier like him. You don't know what really happened. Maybe she wanted to get screwed by him."

"This is a pointless discussion," Lisa said, exasperated.

Then there was a silence between them.

When the air still did not clear between Louise and Lisa, Louise finally turned to Lilly. "I know that feeling," Louise said to Lilly.

"What feeling?" Lisa asked.

"I'm talking to Lilly," Louise said. "Lilly, I understand why you are the way you are," she said. "I feel that way lots of times. You're with people and they don't see you. You try to connect and find love, but you can't because people don't see you there. You don't exist. You feel it's just awful to be you. It's not because you're sick, but because you don't connect with anybody."

"I was just watching the rain," Lilly said. "I didn't mean to be rude."

"I know that feeling, too, Louise," Lisa said now, softly. "I do, Louise."

"I have ago-ra-phobia, Lilly," Louise suddenly blurted. "It's my ago-ra-phobia that got me here. Lisa knows about it, don't you, Lisa?"

Lisa nodded, looking relieved. Louise was including her again.

"I stayed in my apartment all day," Louise went on. "I couldn't connect with anybody. I got fat, too." She stopped, but only for a short breath. "Did you know that a certain famous West Village painter used to come to paint my portrait in my apartment? I modeled all the time for him. I was thinking of being a real model. Until I got ago-ra-phobia. I was sure I would get treated for it here, but when they give me passes, I get as far as the hospital basement cafeteria before I can't face going out of the building. I found the candy machines down in the basement last week when I was there. They are the best candy machines in the whole city, including movie theaters and train stations."

"Are you finished?" Lisa quipped, irritated at Louise again. "Oh, God, what more could you possibly have to add about some candy machines in the basement cafeteria, Louise?"

"I just wanted to tell Lilly I hope she gets passes soon," Louise said defensively. "And, well, oh . . . that kind of vending machine is becoming a thing of the past. This discussion makes me sad. I miss those old candy machines they used to have. Remember Mallomars?"

"I think that's a cookie, not a candy, Louise," Lisa said.

Lilly listened to the light fall of rain outside the window as Lilly and Louise bickered again. She imagined the mesmerizing hands of Patty Hearst's abductor, his criminal cock stealing into her sex with the force of a beating hand. He was fierce and seductive in the pictures, like the cobra on his leather belt. She felt the dread of the sleepless night in front of her. The recurring dream of her own faceless criminal When he possessed her, her orgasms were humiliating, mortifying, but she filled, and her nightmares of large, remonstrating women annihilated, destroyed her. She was with Lisa and Louise now, she thought, and even as they continued to argue, she felt safer. She could stay up again tonight, wait for morning when they would all come back to the lounge and sit together. She listened harder to the rain, losing herself to its soft patter as it fell on the trees below them. Spring was almost over whenever she heard the sound of a hard rain, she thought. The fiercer rainfall always signaled the end of spring and its drizzles, that the weather would be heating up. It was summer's approaching warning, making those whooshing, drumming sounds. Soon the sun would be burning down every day, she was thinking, and a more serious heat would come with the more serious rain. The water from the sky would get even heavier, pouring onto the city rooftops, cascading and growing into streams that looked like clear and translucent snakes slivering down gutters. She remembered the damp heat of Bedford, how different it had been from the city. When the spring rain came, it melted the snow, and water started flowing drip by drip, running together and forming rivulets, then rivulets ran into wider streams, and the water leapt joyously down the forest paths. Then Lilly remembered the moon outside her window in Bedford, the sight of the floating white moon disc in the pink Westchester clouds.

She wouldn't know how to find the moon here. It seemed to always be vanishing into the unsettled nights when she looked for it outside her hospital window.

"Louise, what were the results of your beautician test?" Lilly heard Lisa and Louise, and she listened now to them instead. Her private thoughts were growing more unfocused and scattered.

"Haven't gotten them back yet, cupcake," Louise was answering Lisa. "I'm not going to think about it. I'm bad at tests, you know. I have massive 'deficit of concentration.' Even Dr. Leach says so."

"Anyone can take tests. But who can design hair like you?" Lisa said, and Lilly looked at her. *Despite her petulance, Lisa had a warm heart*, Lilly thought.

"You're a real artist, Louise," Lisa was saying.

Louise cleared her throat, uplifted by Lisa's warmth. "These are all my children, you know," Louise said, addressing both Lilly and Lisa now. "Well, they're not my actual children, but I call them my children. All my kids on this psycho floor. I love them all so much. I want them to know that someone loves them and accepts them for exactly who they are. All my life I just want them to know that someone who isn't like them can still love and accept them. That is a lot of the reason I am so open to everyone, anyone, here on the floor, and in life. When I meet someone and I like them, I like them for themselves. The rest of that stuff is just . . . cosmetic . . . I mean." Louise paused and then Lisa was nodding approvingly at her, and she went on: "Whoever you are, however you ID yourself, if I like you I like you. It makes me angry and sad and sick that there are people out there going through exactly what my Uncle Keith did to me."

"What did he do?" Lisa asked, concerned now. "Did Uncle Keith take advantage of you? I mean . . . did he molest you, Louise? Oh, Louise I'm so sorry, I didn't know."

"No, no!" Louise cried. "Uncle Keith made me come to the hospital. He made me become a mental patient! He's the one who put me in here! I feel for all the people who are told they are crazy. They're being told by the people that are supposed to love them that there is something wrong with them, that they are incomplete or flawed somehow. I want to take them in my arms and hug them long and deep and tell them that there is *nothing* wrong with them. Whatever you are it's okay. It's okay with me. I don't want there to be anyone out there who doesn't have *someone* who says, 'I love you for who you are. I see you. So please have a good night, my kitten.' I want a good night for all my pets. I want them to feel warm, soft kisses, too."

As Louise finished, breathless, she reached to touch Lilly. Her right hand softly rubbed and stroked Lilly's arm. "Honey, you're so beautiful and sensitive, you're like a Russian princess, I swear . . . ," she said.

Lilly tugged hard against Louise's hold, trying hard not to reveal her panic. Then Lilly's head was spinning, as if it were filling with some intoxicant that had penetrated her.

"Jesus Christ, Louise," Lisa said. "You're scaring her."

"I just touched her!" Louise said, quickly withdrawing her hand from Lilly's arm. "I'm sorry, Lilly, don't be scared. I should get my hairstyling equipment for you, Lilly. Should I get my salon out, Lisa? I used to do Marie's hair all the time. Lilly's a little taller than Marie, but don't they look alike? That dark look, very chic, sexy. You have no reason in the world to feel bad about yourself, Lilly," Louise said, louder, as if calling Lilly back to her from faraway. "You'll see. Believe me, your 'condition' will make nice lines on your face, you will be so intriguing. Play it up, darling. You will always be mysterious. Maybe I should try a mod style, short cut with bangs on Lilly, too, Lisa. Remember that was the style I used on Marie?"

"I told you about Marie," Lisa said to Lilly now. "You remind me of her, too, Lilly."

"You're thinking of Marie and her files because you know Wendy Wilson's leaving tomorrow," Louise said to Lisa.

"No, I wasn't," Lisa answered. "I don't think about Marie anymore. I found one of her old files in my room, and I thought Lilly would like it."

"Wendy Wilson's leaving tomorrow," Louise said. "She didn't give anyone her home phone number either. Just like Marie."

Lilly was able to nod back now, relieved that they were finally thinking of someone else, the focus of all their energy shifting to a departed patient named Marie. It happened a lot on the ward, the sudden ghosts reappearing through the likenesses between patient and patient. Lisa had started to tell Lilly about Marie last week when they were watching the late-night news. Lilly knew nothing more about Marie than that she had been discharged in March, she hadn't phoned the ward, she had vanished into her outside life.

"There's a game, Lilly," Lisa began explaining now to Lilly. "It's called alternative files. I played it a lot with Marie. See, I have Marie's alternative files. I gave them to you, didn't I? Where'd you put them?"

"There," Lilly said, turning her head toward the window.

"I miss Marie, too, Lisa," Louise said as Lilly remembered the folder she had placed on the sill. "I used to do Marie's hair nice and firm for her," Louise said. "Lilly, I have those big curlers, you know the old-fashioned kind? No-nonsense curlers, I mean, the kind you can definitely rely on."

"It's easy," Lisa said, cutting Louise off. "Look, they're in there writing up all sorts of conspirational theories in the nursing station. The hall nurses I mean. We're the people who always get written about but Marie kept her own files, on herself and all the patients. She said people should know who they aren't nothing, what they are is *different.* Which means they are *something* and not what the staff say they are. We called them the alternative files. She kept them, lie a journal so the staff wouldn't know she had them. She left them for me to keep when she left."

"She gave them to you, Lisa?" Louise asked. "She gave them away?"

Lilly now took the "file" from the sill. Lisa's fingers were gentle, pulling it from Lilly's anxious hands.

"Marie was brilliant, "Lisa said to Lilly, continuing to ignore Louise. "She had the IQ of a frightening genius, but she was schizophrenic. I loved the way she said things but you had to listen hard to what she said, she jumbled her words sometimes."

Lisa settled the folder calmly on her lap. "Look, go to the nursing station when Dina is there, Lilly." Lisa explained now. . "She's the little nurse, the one with the great legs; tiny, petite. You'll see all the nurses in there writing notes on us. Take a peek. They sit in the nursing station eating lunch and do it. They have the air-conditioner on already, and they wear sweaters which makes little sense. I think it's not to show their potential mates—all those young residents they hope to marry—too much of their bare skin, like those Jewish women at the wailing wall who cover themselves with shawls."

"But the sweaters sure show their breasts." Louise interjected. "How do you know what they write about us anyway? Maybe they're writing reports about how special and divine we are?"

"Who is *not* going to see you as a nothing on the outside?" Lisa's voice was strident. "Once a mental patient, always a mental patient. All the people you meet once you're out of here will tell you that you were just being lazy and self-indulgent, unless they think you are really crazy like Spia. It is a hopeless hell, like you're being cremated alive because you become an idea someone else has about what it means to be a mental patient instead of a real person. And then you have to cope with your own self-respect."

"God, that's awful," Louise said now.

Lilly pulled her knees up to her chin, sitting up on the couch and imagining herself stiff and still as a building, vanishing into an invisible dimension in space. *Was this what Lisa meant?* she wondered. She didn't understand what Lisa meant, yet she felt it completely. It was some self-consuming, emotionally bottomless place of identity where one was only a vacuum; she knew this place—where one is only a receiver for unspecified signals and transmissions in the air. Being a nothing was a treacherous existence.

After a few minutes, Lisa was silent, too, as if contemplating the greater depths of the situation.

Then Louise leaned closer toward Lilly. "Lilly, let me tell you something," she said. Her eyes seemed to jiggle in their sockets. "Every suffering person has been assigned someone, by God, to save them."

"Lilly's Jewish," Lisa said.

"It's not about religion, Lisa. It's about karma," Louise said.

"I'm half-Jewish," Lisa said to Lilly. "But I love Mass."

"I've never been to a Mass," Lilly said, talking at the same time she wanted to disappear.

"We have one in Westport. Christmas morning I attend St. Bartholomew's near the Westport Country Club for Mass."

"Is that where you're from?"

"My parents live there. I grew up there," Lisa responded.

"Doesn't Paul Newman live there?" Louise asked.

"Oh, Louise," Lisa smiled more patiently now. "What are we going to do with you, Louise? Tell me. What are we going to do?"

"You can love me," Louise said. "Love and acceptance are all I want from anyone."

Now it felt uncomfortable in the room again, and Lilly shifted on the couch. She thought of walking away like Frank, into her room. Maybe she could try to write again in the notebook, she thought.

But then Lisa opened the manila file and pulled out the newspaper clipping, unfolding it. Lilly saw it was titled "Leonard." It was filled with Marie's illegible notes along with a clipping from the *New York Times*.

"Leonard is the son of a very renowned chemist and engineer, you know. His father helped discover the transistor for Bell Laboratories." *Lisa's like a cup of unskimmed information,* Lilly thought, something wildly stirred so that filmy layers settled on top, and unknown particles, curdled and scattered, swam around in the skim.

Lilly looked down at the clipping as Lisa continued talking. The black-and-white photo in the newspaper portrayed white flames. Blurry images of people as they ran, scattering all over the Grand Central stairway. Soft-focused faces. Lilly could almost hear their screams, but could not make out individuals.

The caption under the photo read, "Fire trucks and ambulances on the scene inside Grand Central Station where a Kodak picture exploded. A gunman was apprehended as hundreds fled."

"Leonard was *different,*" Lisa was saying. "He's pretty much a straight, handsome man if you look at him. He can't handle his feelings, and he can't deal with anyone or anything except flat abstract theories. One day Leonard takes some acid another Columbia student gives him. So he gets a gun," Lisa was continuing. "A rifle from a friend's hunting case, and goes to Grand Central Station and *Bang! Bang! Bang!* He fires at a twenty-by-twenty-foot photograph behind a glass shield. I think it was a blown-up 'Kodak moment' of a picture-perfect family lying in a hammock somewhere, on vacation in the Caribbean, but with all these wires and electric circuits behind it to light it up over the station. Leonard's lawyers have made him plead 'temporary insanity' and 'under the influence of drugs,' but he is a lost soul, you know."

Lisa was finished. She moved to the set of armchairs by the TV. The news was on by then, and some cartoons on other channels, and she seemed spent, having finally told Lilly the whole story of Leonard.

Louise stood up. She began stretching out in a series of arm lifts and knee bends.

Lilly twisted around on the couch. She looked at the seat where Leonard sat last evening. The rain was still splashing, and it made the sky prematurely dark when Lilly looked back outside. The long evening had already begun.

₪

After dinner, Lilly was back on the couch, looking down at the rushing FDR Drive in the night. The lounge was quiet and still. Frank didn't come back to the table where two other patients had started the nightly backgammon tournament now. Lisa and Louise told Lilly over the meal—Hawaiian pineapple chicken and green beans—that they would join her again in the lounge.

Her dreams might be better tonight, Lilly was thinking. And she was so tired now, she would sleep easily.

But by midnight Lilly heard a harrowing wail down the corridor. She rushed and looked out the door, expecting something terrible might have happened. Down the corridor it was

Louise banging at the north side's phone booth with her fist, then kicking at the phone booth's door. A posse of staff raced for the corridor.

"You know who you are, Uncle Keith!" Louise was screaming into the phone. "FUCK YOU. I hope to God I never see you. I understand why you did what you did, but this is a violation of my life. FUCK YOU a thousand times over. I hope you're proud of yourself. It's gotta feel pretty good, fucking up the life of someone you don't even FUCKING KNOW." She was screaming as if she were getting choked, and soon the staff was hanging up the phone for her, telling her in firm voices, "You're here to get control. . . ."

Lilly heard the now-familiar struggle as they dragged Louise through to the quiet room. Then the quiet door slammed. The noise was shut out. But by then another patient had a fit and had kicked a floor lamp to the floor and busted its glass bulb. Lilly could see it glistening in the distance. In a few minutes, a staff member hurriedly came to retrieve the shatters, unplugged the lamp, and left it there for the custodian to pick up in the morning. And the corridor's floor was a vacant strip again—desolate and deserted.

₪

"What are your plans to do to me?" Lilly asked Dr. Burkert the next morning. She was sitting opposite him inside his office at the south corridor. A clear blue morning was approaching, and the light was warm. The air was still stuffy, slightly dusty hospital air, but it contained the faint scent of the tulips and spruce trees outside in the hedges and flower beds. Lilly thought she heard a gardener's hose below the window.

"Is that what you think? That we make plans 'to do' to people here?" There were only folders and loose pinkish forms on Dr. Burkert's desk. Nothing personal of his was in the room at all, neither on the windowsill nor on the desk. There were no houseplants nor family photos. The sparseness of the office made it feel more like a shaft. The drawers were dented, aluminum, and plain. "Plans for discharge are something we decide together," he said.

Dr. Burkert's a disciplined man, Lilly thought, as his neatness and sandy hair showed. He now seemed dangerous, not the same as he had in her room the first days, his foreign accent not a link to Helen, but an echo from the photographs in her mother's old albums to classify along with the invisible persecutors and phantoms, the British Tommies. *He isn't very warm,* she thought, despite the meaning of his words. And now he seemed always impatient, different from the first night he saw her. His tone was too careful. She had to leave behind everything solid, bleeding, and carnal in her dreams or writing, *in her own country,* she thought, like Helen once had to. Lilly, the person, was now devoid of passion, a thing being blown through the dust.

Caroline had called into her room to tell her she was ready for her first real session in Dr. Burkert's office. Caroline had said Lilly was to go herself without an escort this morning, directly after breakfast. Now Lilly checked herself again. Dr. Burkert was pulling her into some trap, making her think of her mother. Nothing could make her trust him or believe he wasn't there to judge and look down on her.

"Are you all right?" Dr. Burkert asked her.

Lilly turned in the old chair to face him square on. She firmed her shoes on the floor but said nothing.

"You're very guarded, you know," Dr. Burkert said. "Like now, for example. Are you afraid to tell me what you are feeling?"

"This office is cold," she said. "And you don't care what I feel."

"So I'm cold, too?" Dr. Burkert said.

"I would like to know how long you're going to keep me here."

"As short as possible. I understand that it's hard to be in the hospital."

"Perhaps," Lilly said but then stopped, aware of the sweat that was just beginning to coat her neck and her legs. She fidgeted for a few seconds, picking at loose threads on the belt strap of her jeans. She made herself swallow so that the knot that was burning in her stomach would be cooled and unwind. Then she imagined herself out of the room. She was a vaporous entity streaming invisibly past him and out through a small crack under the window into the spring sunlight.

"Are you feeling the discomfort now? The nurses tell me you seem very uncomfortable, you look frightened."

"No," she lied.

"I'm sorry you feel you can't tell me what you feel," he said. Lilly tore at a cuticle on her thumb. "Well, I can't," she said.

"I see."

"Good."

"Your mother called the ward. She would like to come to the hospital. Would you be willing to talk to me about your mother? She keeps calling us."

"What?" Lilly startled, alarmed. "What did she tell you?"

"It's fine if you'd like us to keep your mother from visiting. This is your time to sort out things. I want you to feel safe." Dr. Burkert's formal eyes softened on Lilly as he spoke carefully.

Lilly didn't understand his kindness or his tenderness. It pulled at her as if she had her head against his shoulder, and his arms were around her and they were falling asleep together, ready to share some terrible night dream. In the hospital, intimacy came fast as a train. It was like being in a passenger compartment traveling at a deafening speed. Everything passed by rapidly, too, but from out the window as if she were seated in the compartment, only watching. Her thoughts were racing away from him, trying to tug away from his grasp.

"I want to know if there wouldn't be any more examinations," she found herself saying. "They took me up from the emergency room that first night and the nurse violated me."

"Are you sure that's what happened?"

"Yes," she said.

"Do you remember why I ordered the physical exam for you?"

"My mother is always out of control like that," she said, struggling against the momentum she could not stop, but failing. "My mother can't be trusted to tell you the truth. She has hysteria."

"I see."

"She's hysterical all the time. She's really very ill and dangerous."

"I think you mean she is dangerous to you," he said.

The thought sent her into spinning confusion. Meanwhile, a chaos of trampling feet were lining up, waiting for the dining room door to open for lunch. Voices were yammering louder and louder that things were disappearing from their rooms; a thief was in the hall, taking things in their drawers. Lisa was demanding a thorough search of all the patients' rooms. Then a shriek sliced the air, belonging to a female whose voice Lilly didn't recognize and who was screaming, "I want to die! I'm not safe here!"

Dr. Burkert stood from his desk. "Please excuse me. I need to check on this." He circled her chair, and she watched him as he went out into the hall to see what was happening.

Alone in the office, released from having to talk, Lilly felt grateful to whoever might be the thief for sparing her, giving her the time now to collect herself. She straightened in her chair, angry with herself. She would have to be more constantly diligent, she told herself. If she weren't more careful, she could be turned into fluid parts. She was telling Dr. Burkert too much. He could disassemble her.

Then Helen moved through her thoughts like the faint slap of a hand and Lilly was shaking, guilty for what she said about Helen. Dr. Burkert couldn't understand, but Lilly didn't understand either, she thought now. It was as if something were following her and took Helen's form, like a threat wrapping around her.

"I'm so sorry," Dr. Burkert said, reentering the room minutes later. "I had to take care of that disturbance on the hall. This was a lot for one session, I think, so why don't we stop for today and pick this up tomorrow?"

But Lilly was already caving in. She couldn't hold on; it was as if he had undone some secret hinge inside her.

ןﬗ

That evening in her room, too tired to think anymore, Lilly stood at the secured window, wanting to lean out, to sip in the after-rain night air. Two orderlies were carrying a body on a stretcher toward the emergency room inside the medical hospital, a distance away. A sick man, the first one Lilly saw these long weeks. She watched his body struggling on the stretcher, as if he were keeping some fight alive to explain who he was against the engulfment of his illness. She saw him moving on the stretcher, lugged farther off into darkness, then vanishing down the ramp that led to the emergency room entrance.

Lilly listened for some hall sounds, but the whole place was so quiet.

Suddenly, Lilly was thinking of Jane, her roommate, and a wave of anguish flowed through her. They used to be able to talk for hours, pass wordless feelings to one another. Even when Lilly was afraid of talking. Jane would always contribute the

striking presence of her corn-colored hair, the graceful manners she had as she sat cross-legged on the rod-iron divan in
their Little Italy apartment, patiently saying "Uh-huh" as they
talked so that Lilly believed Jane understood Lilly's exasperation about everything.

Just thinking about Jane, she could get away from Dr.
Burkert and his intrusive questions with their threat of disintegrating her. Lilly wondered what it would feel like to walk
in their apartment now, how it would feel. She wondered if it
could ever be the same, if she could fit back in anywhere, even
with Jane. Outside the hospital room's window, the city seemed
like a hazy country floating in some intangible interval between
then and now.

Maybe her life before the hospital had been a dream of
sorts, she thought. It seemed so far away now, like someone
else's life. Everything was changed. Everything that existed on
the other side of the window—Jane, Helen, her father, college,
thoughts of the past—now seemed insubstantial, leaving a hole
deep inside her where emptiness crept in. If she went out into
the city streets, she thought, she would be faced with millions of
people wanting nothing to do with her anymore.

She stayed by the window, squinting, though there was no
moonlight nor streetlights. And she wondered if she were any
different from the body on the stretcher she'd just seen carried
in the night.

When Lilly fell asleep in her hospital bed that night, she
dreamed she was home in Little Italy, and Jane was reading a
phone book to her. They were trying to look up numbers to call
because they had killed a rat, but maybe it was a man, and they
had to get rid of the corpse.

She awoke to the lonely shock of her hospital room.

₪

That morning at 6 a.m., Lilly was already up, washing her face in the tiny sink. She was in her nightgown, and she pulled her blue jeans and T-shirt on rapidly as she heard the footsteps outside her door—patients racing from their rooms, down the corridor.

Flashing red lights and shouting filled the halls. Lilly let the door to her room shut behind her as she scrambled with the crowd to the window in the center lounge. A group of staff were policing the area, pushing through to get closer to the shattered glass.

Lilly had heard nothing in her room of the glass breaking.

Patients were kneeling on the leather couch, but staff members were shouting at them to clear off it. Dangerous broken glass from the window was all over the couch which lay directly under its sill, and in the windless morning, shards with knifelike edges and some small glittering particles, too, made the whole couch seem lighted.

"Please get away from the window!" Caroline was shouting.

What lay below, outside them, was uncertain. The patients were trying to make sense of the patrolmen and security guards circled around in an area outside the garden gates, in a gully between the gates and the FDR.

There was a low haze of city morning. The sun hadn't risen yet, and the gathering police squad threw no shadows. Somewhere, Lilly thought, as she struggled to look out, beyond the inside commotion of patients and nurses in the lounge, was the shadow of what lay on the ground, but she couldn't see it. And she dreaded seeing it.

Then Lilly heard Caroline shouting out in the chaotic confusion inside the crowding room: "Please let's gather around now!"

"Who was it?" A patient pulled at the silence.

Other voices rose. "Who? Was it Leonard? I saw him go in here."

Patients were ushered away from the debris quickly, and Lilly was tapped gently on her shoulder by an aide, telling her to get away from the window. She followed the other patients into the South Lounge.

"Yes," Lilly heard Caroline say, walking beside another patient in the group, "Yes . . . it was Leonard."

There was a stone quiet in the South Lounge, patients fumbling through broken conversations about what had happened.

Lilly looked at the shaft of yellow lamplight that had bathed Leonard as he read or talked in the evenings. She only knew him for a short time under that light, she thought, too short a time for her to feel what she was feeling. But a thick doom gripped her.

Chapter Nine

Black water trickled between the flagstone tiles of the hospital's courtyard. It was afternoon, the same day. An emergency meeting had been called at eight that same morning to briefly discuss the suicide, and then postponed. Cardboard and wooden boards were secured tightly on the gaping hole in the center lounge's window, but it would be hours before the window could be fully repaired, so the lounge wasn't safe. The lounge looked torn apart, though Leonard had only pulled out the lamp and crashed its base against the window glass. Staff and patients and scrambled through it, disrupting it's orderly array of chairs and game tables. The patients were rushed out to other places in the hall again; most of them were listlessly and aimlessly wandering the corridors, or searching for therapists, asking where their doctors were. Gravity deadened the air—shock and silence—and it seemed like each patient was painlessly alone. There was no communion among them, as if the incident had made them into separate beings again, back into the loneliness of illness and hopelessness. Finally, by afternoon, the whole patient community was shepherded off the hall and taken down to the garden. Lilly felt herself pulled into a long string of blackening hours, bereft and empty, and she didn't know why.

Now the garden air swelled with after-rain moisture. There was still hardly any sun, as if the gloomy dawn were still with them, and the sun had never risen at all. Lilly looked helplessly around the garden.

Wetted flakes of city ash—flecks that looked like black scarabs—tarnished the plump, assiduously pruned flowers inside the few patches of green enclosed by a square rod-iron fence. On the other side were long and heavy gates overlooking the highway, an ocean sound. But, it was the roar of cars traveling on the FDR Drive to the south.

Theresa was chasing the sounds, losing her loafers as she raced around the yard. Her white ankle socks dirtied and tore on the stones.

"Look," Lisa said to Lilly now. "Theresa is trying to reach Nirvana."

Lisa was sitting next to Lilly on the bench. Other patients were seated now, too, on the painted green benches inside the enclosed area.

Lilly shifted on her bench, disturbed.

"Lilly, are you doing all right?" Lisa asked. Lisa's hair seemed to float in the muggy air, its strands brown feathers. A small, tickling wind made the mugginess feel thicker. "Are you okay?"

"Sure," Lilly said.

"My mother and father were coming for a session this afternoon. We were going to talk about my discharge," Lisa went on. "Fuck a duck. With this thing going on on the hall after Leonard, I'm sure it got cancelled."

"Fuck is right," Lilly said. She tried again to listen.

"Come to my room when we finish here, Lilly. We can talk about things, if you like."

"Good," Lilly said. "*Yes.*"

Beverly was seated alone on a bench appearing to read a novel, a short distance away. But she looked up every few minutes, scrutinizing the patients. It was the first time Lilly had seen the nurse since she had examined Lilly that first evening of admission. Beverly appeared shorter and older. But the rest of her was the same. Her tank top as before, too tight. Her round, lawn-colored eyes, cold. Bands of matching green eye shadow brushed on their lids. Lilly wondered if the nurse still smelled of department-store makeup counters and brand-name talc. Beverly's man-sized arms and hands looked portentous— transformative material for Lilly's anxious dreams tonight, Lilly feared, strong mother-arms or the weapons of an overwhelming perpetrator.

You can take me to the principal's office and teach me a good lesson, Lilly thought in silence. *Take me to the police, your locked bedroom.* The lines swimming in her head must have been from some porno magazine she had seen of horrible, luring schoolmistresses. But then Lilly only wanted to look harder at Beverly, as if drawn unwittingly to a wound, or a scab that had only partially healed, and now itched, begging to be touched by clandestine strokes of Lilly's fingers, unnoticed. And she was flirting precipitously with the nurse, with her inner thoughts. She wondered if Beverly had the same penetrating, horrid eyes.

"Lilly?" Lisa was speaking to her again. "What's going on with you, Lilly?"

Lilly didn't answer.

Then, as if hearing Lilly's thoughts, Beverly turned a page in her paperback novel on the bench. She crossed her muscular legs, and her eyes darted a sullen glance at Lilly.

"Lilly?" Lisa touched Lilly lightly on her arm. "Tell me what you're thinking."

"Nothing." Shaken, Lilly snapped her head away from the nurse.

"I don't care about her," Lisa said. "You care what they think about you too much. Are you thinking about Leonard? You're so intense."

Lilly glanced up at the sky through a hole in one of the low, iron-gray clouds. Then, still shaken, her eyes fell back down to watch the other patients disperse around the courtyard. But within a few silent seconds, Lilly was pulled back toward Beverly. The nurse had gone back to her paperback novel.

In the distance, through a corner of one eye, Lilly caught the sight of a male patient talking to himself by the garden fence overlooking the highway. His wide shoulders absorbed the little bit of sunlight, and he was shining in the gray, muddy light. There was a light fog over the day, and the figure, tall and big-shouldered, reminded her of Leonard.

"The cookie-dough-flavored ice cream at Peppermint Patty's is the best choice if you get a pass soon, Lilly," Lisa began chattering absentmindedly. "I went there and ordered it with Louise from the fifth floor.... I'm just saying.... I'm just trying to talk about something cheerful for a change. I don't want to think so hard...."

Lilly lowered her eyes to the soil and flagstone below them. She watched Lisa cross her shoes.

The wind flicked at the pages of Beverly's unread paperback, and soon the nurse was loudly calling to one of the hospital aides: "Sandra, get Theresa to stop that now. Pick up her loafers and put them on. Come on, this isn't a football field. Why is she running around like that?"

"'Live each day as if it's the first day of your life,'" Lisa went on.

Lilly said vacantly, "Sure, sure."

"That is Louise's daily chant. Did you ever see *Godspell?*" Lisa asked.

"I don't think so. No, actually," Lilly said.

"'Oh dear Lord, each day I pray,'" Lisa sang, but now Lisa had tears in her eyes, and she brushed at a fallen leaf on her dress. "I don't think you're really listening. Where's your head, Lilly?"

Lilly turned to stare at the man by the gates. He was reminding her now of her father, the way he looked buried within himself. He was struggling to light a rain-wet cigarette with his gold lighter, talking to himself again as Leonard did on the hall, thin lips muttering in slow movements. Lilly thought she heard the words he was muttering to himself, as she might hear a buzz in the wind, almost like a crow sound. They seemed to touch her, and she thought about what the dimensions of an invisible stadium of ghosts might be—how one could measure the space the dead took up by their spirits, and how the living could sometimes be like ghosts, half in that other sphere. She could feel the man's baggy clothes on his reduced body, his words no longer communicating to this world, because she had developed a supernatural sense for the spirits inside withered bodies. It was one talent her father bestowed on her with his illness, the ability to search past the foul scents of his body, his brain damage, for the spirit she remembered he once had been. There was a small transistor radio playing "Catch the Wind," as, becoming fearful, Lilly, resisted a pull to reach with her eyes back at Beverly.

"Don't look at that guy," Lisa sharply said to Lilly again.

"I thought he was Leonard," Lilly said.

"Leonard was a sick man," Lisa said. "He had a gun. Do you think I am misleading you?"

Lilly felt her leg muscles pinch, and she kept her eyes on the back of the stranger Lisa was describing, as if the sight could muffle the disturbing words Lisa was saying, but she did not want Lisa to think she wasn't listening.

"I guess you're right," Lilly said, but she continued watching the man at the gate, wondering how a body that large and bulky could not, by sheer force, break through the gates. She imagined him for a moment pulling apart the bars with his bare hands—hands she would never have, muscles and stature she would never possess. She tried to read into his swaying body, but his aimless motion began to disorient her.

The sight of his knees, his construction boots filled her with fear.

"Hey," Lisa said now, tenderly. "Lilly, what's wrong. Oh, Lilly . . ."

Lilly turned away from the sight of the disturbed man, her mouth finally opening, though she couldn't talk, her eyes grasping onto Lisa.

An aide, brandishing two fallen penny loafers, was trying to catch Theresa, who was wet with manic drooling, giggling, jumping, and skipping around the circled garden like a lighted firecracker. Beverly suddenly stood up and strode over, looming large in her concern, and sweeping Lilly into her trajectory. Her imposing girth made Lilly remember Helen when it was cold outside in Bedford, driving down to where Lilly had stood shivering on the driveway, waiting for the school bus to come. Her mother would open the door to the Ford Mustang, waving Lilly into the heated car with its red leather seats and AM radio. Her mother's hands had once been as warm as the gusts from the car heater, like blankets on Lilly's freezing cheeks. Then Lilly was thinking of the statue of the Mother Mary in the baptistery and, as if the bulb had been shaken, it stirred, conducting an electricity of emotions and sensations through Lilly. Everything was suddenly threatening: the rainy mist, the odors of city, and the garden. She didn't want anything to happen, but a tension was building within her.

She watched Beverly as she approached the aide and the manic Theresa. Theresa had fallen to the flagstone now, her skirt had torn, and a flash of her cotton girl's underwear, speckled with pebbly garden soil, glistened under the sparse sunlight.

"Theresa," she heard Beverly say, and Beverly's face became strict, her hand pulling up the girl who was now struggling to stand. Theresa was still giggling, and her drool was falling on her pants like viscous tears.

Lilly watched them, and, in spite of herself, Lilly was pulling Beverly tight against her to fill her emptiness. Lilly didn't want to feel anything, but a heat passed through her, a warm breath like a kiss. Then a debasing sexual electricity overwhelmed her, as if a tangle of exposed wires and failed transmissions were running through her in a horrible, widening destruction. The heat became a voracious surge; a flaming ignited Lilly's feelings and Lilly's body.

Lilly doubled over, clutching her midriff. It was a catastrophe—this sudden letting-out, against her will. Eye to eye, filled by a woman she feared and hated and didn't want to be near. No, she couldn't have come, she told herself, but she had orgasmed, a tortured spasm and spill, and there were trembles within her now. It was because Lilly cannot love at all, she thought. Lilly could only love a behemoth, she was thinking, and not even know whether it is a man or woman, and what was Lilly? Hip to knee, she was only a vibrating pole of flesh, and now—Lilly was nothing. She wanted to push her fist between her thighs, into the hole of herself, dig her fist where the intense upheaval in her stomach was turning into a mix of sex and incontinence. The confusing trembling surged yet again in her genitals, and she was horrified, beyond any shame—as if she had expelled a miscarriage through her bowels.

"All right, people, it's time to go in!" a staff member was shouting.

"People, let's stay together. We're going to have another community meeting. If you could all just remain together . . . ," the nurse was calling.

Beverly was standing and signaling the other patients with her powerful arm, trying to move them into a group in the center of the garden. Lilly sought the eyes of the man by the gate. But it was Beverly who held the exit door open and stood protectively, one foot outside in the courtyard, but one foot keeping the door ajar for the others. Her shadow gave off a warmth, and Lilly started to sink into it again.

Then Lilly pulled herself away, disoriented, her head filling with confusion and panic. Leonard's suicide entered her thoughts, like a pull into blissful extinction.

Beverly was alert to Lilly's behavior, gesturing at Lilly, and then Lilly knew she could not run toward the gates. Beverly was still bringing the patients into a shielded circle by the exit door, and her forceful arm was a sharper order in the air, calling Lilly to join the group of patients.

Finally, Lilly shambled to the courtyard door. She was splitting apart from the convergence of the two awful events she did not comprehend—the numbing orgasms and the plunge of a soul on the opposite pole of life's spectrum into a different kind of oblivion.

Lilly followed the group into the building as Beverly let the garden exit door slam shut. The elevator doors opened as she slowly led the group into the elevator car, back to safety.

The elevators finally closed.

"All right, we're moving," another nurse said as the elevator began its ascension.

₪

"Please, let's start," Caroline's familiar husky voice reached out to the circle of seated patients in the lounge. "First I would like to tell you, as a group, exactly what happened. At four o'clock this morning, Leonard took his own life. He found a way to smash the window, and he jumped. We need to assure you the staff is here for all of you. We know it seemed as if the staff weren't there for Leonard, whom most of you know well from our floor. Louise, you seem very upset."

Lilly, seated across the room, tried to make out Louise's face, but her stomach and bowels were blazing. Some horrible guilt was seizing her, torturing her from within, a psychic flame, as if from a candle consuming its own periphery, destroying its own center.

"What?" Louise asked in a high-pitched voice.

"You seem distressed, Louise," Caroline said.

"I knew Leonard," a male patient interjected. But Lilly didn't look toward him, or try to determine who was speaking now. She had already removed herself from the crowded room of patients.

Leonard sped through Lilly's imagination again: falling, shooting into a shattering explosion of a person, but what person?

"The staff wants to talk to all of you about what happened," Caroline was persevering.

The drone of collective voices blended together until Louise shook into hysterics.

"Oh my God, did you see it? Oh, my God!" she cried.

"Yes, he jumped," Caroline's cautious, slowly enunciated explanation was continuing." We had him on watch, but there was a change in shift at midnight. He waited until the early hours of morning, and then he broke the window."

Leonard's life was now vanishing into the thick, muggy gray outside. Lilly imagined him as he tumbled down in the air almost noiselessly, like a wind that only makes itself known and seen in relation to some other object—a treetop as it lashes, underbrush as it rustles, leaves swirling up from the ground. . . .

Suddenly, Lilly wanted to flee from the circle, to go back to her own room and sleep. She was so tired, *fagged out*, she thought, remembering how she had described her fatigue to herself in the Northern Westchester hospital lobby the night her father fell, and she heard a thud below her in the bathroom. Remembering how she waited for her mother on a bare wooden bench in the hospital lobby, when her mother was upstairs visiting her father and she was alone, the sunlight piercing through some distant churchly windows with a celestial glow. *If I am so tired and there is still so much tragedy to go through, I could curl up here, roll onto my side, tuck a hand below my chin and just sleep,* she had thought. *If there is still that much tragedy to go through, why couldn't I take a short nap, rest up—"snooze" would be the word my father might have used, like the cartoon boys and girls in the funnies when all the zzz's are trailing from their drawn skulls.*

"Do people have fantasies about doing what Leonard did?" Caroline was persisting.

Lilly looked for Dr. Burkert at his usual spot, a swivel chair, in the corner by the phonograph, but it was empty. Desperately she made a harder effort to listen to what Caroline was saying, but the voices in the meeting were undifferentiated, as if from one bulk of body.

"This has been a very upsetting incident for all of us," she now heard Caroline say. "And I want everyone in the group to have some time to think about what happened. You will all be talking to your doctors about how you feel. But please come and seek out any staff member if you feel like you need to talk about it at any time."

Lilly looked toward Beverly. The nurse looked at her with concern. And then a feeling began, first in Lilly's fingers, joints lightly burning.

People were fighting. Arguing, noise, and light expanding.

Then Lilly saw Dr. Burkert. He had slipped in, and his shirt was stained by slashes of lamplight. She wondered where he had been. He was too late.

She saw him approaching her, as if from a dark hole in her vision. The meeting was breaking up.

"Are you all right?" he asked.

Lilly's fingers flew to her face, jittery, rubbing her cheeks, as if smudges had stained them.

"It's 4:45. You have forty-five minutes before dinner. Would you like to talk in my office?"

Lilly felt herself nodding.

He walked ahead of Lilly down the corridor, glancing back at her a few times. He turned the key to his locked office, bending down slightly. "You're agitated. Is there something you are struggling with? You seemed very disturbed by the meeting." He gestured her inside the room.

She watched him turn on the light; the plastic squares in the ceiling were like those in her room. She stepped forward and sat in her usual wooden chair. She felt her own quivering, a prison of trembling. Her hand wanted to hold the bulb again, and only in her imagination she was screaming "Fuck you!" at Dr. Burkert.

"What is it?" Dr. Burkert asked. "Can you tell me?"

Lilly swallowed more and more fiercely to smother her voice. Then she was ranting, but only inside herself. Because she was only air, she thought. Neither language nor emotion could gather together to prevent the inevitable evaporation. They couldn't help her out of this. She felt a growing force pulling her to him. If only he would let her alone—take his eyes and hands with him. *Go away!*

Lilly looked down. But she was wet at the corners of her mouth from holding in her screams. Then she was slipping from the chair, and her hands had to grab for the bulb—she couldn't control them.

A humming wind fluttered at the metal-shuttered window in the tiny office.

Lilly slipped, tripped into darkness. She thought Dr. Burkert would catch her in his arms when she began sliding from her chair to the floor. She almost fell. But she balanced herself and lurched, flinging open the office door, into the corridor.

Lilly ran to her room.

The dinner bell chimed, the night lights of the hall came on for the others clambering toward the dining room. But Lilly's lips were bars, closing tightly on the screams within her, imprisoning her.

מ

When Lilly reached for the desk lamp in her room, its lampshade looked like a little girl's dress, flowing down the lamp stand, gingham and nearly sheer, transparent.

She hurled it and its cord jumped from the socket, whipped through the air, dashing against the window. She threw herself on the bed and turned over on her belly, and the outpouring of tears was worse than the rage. All she felt was her head imploding.

"Okay, young lady, that's enough. We've had enough, do you understand, Lilly?" It was Caroline, standing with another nurse in her room. "Okay, you have two choices here. Let me explain them to you," Caroline went on. "You can get up, get off that bed, and come to the quiet room willingly with the two of us walking you in, nice and calm. Or if you throw another goddamn thing—and I mean this—we're going to do whatever it takes to take you there against your will."

Lilly blinked. The swamp of tears stung. She brushed at her eyes with the back of her hand.

"I'll go," she said, and suddenly her form—the weight of her—seemed to come back, filling out her skeletal frame with real flesh and bone. There was no more of the tantrum welling up to tear at her from inside.

₪

"So we are back here." Dr. Burkert was over Lilly as she stretched under the overhead fluorescent light inside the white seclusion room an hour later. "You lost control again and threw a lamp. It would have been better if you could have spoken with me about what you were feeling."

Lilly looked up. The whiteness of the room was glaring, like a blinding afternoon sun. The nurses had sedated her. She wasn't sure what medicine had forced her into this drowsy heaviness, but her head felt as though it was detached from her body.

"Let her sleep it off," Lilly had heard Caroline say, and then the quiet room door had shut. Lilly didn't know exactly how long she had been lying here. She had walked into the quiet room by her own will, upright and fully dressed, anchored on both sides by more aides. She was still wearing the same blue jeans. They hadn't changed her clothes.

Now she felt a tiny throb and reached for the sore place on her upper arm where the injection had gone in.

"For some patients, coming into the quiet room can bring a sense of control," Dr. Burkert was saying. "You've been here for an hour or so, and you have been sedated."

She didn't answer. Lilly clasped her hands around both her arms, and she remained lying flat on her back. When she looked up she saw Dr. Burkert squatting beside her mattress; his sharp knees and long legs made a lap like a cliff. His hands were on the precipice over his bent knees, watching her.

"I'm sorry this is happening to you," he said. "I know you feel very vulnerable."

Dr. Burkert was quiet now. He waited. She knew he must be thinking; it may take time before she would open up to him. She let the silence blanket her.

The medicine made her head feel floaty, the extreme whiteness of the room was calming her. She could tell him everything that happened in the garden, if she didn't feel him so close to her, she thought. And then, whether from the clouds inside her head, or her muscles that turned soft as butter from the strong medicine, she felt him moving through her. She would have said, *Beverly was there, and I was with her, we were so close, my body became misshapen, I tried to look for a man but I came.* Her mind was in a dream, and Dr. Burkert was suddenly in the dream with her. She could feel him moving through the folds of her imagination. In the dream, there was a young girl abandoned somewhere in a closet, a dirty room with only darkness. Lilly could heard her shrieks from somewhere in the distance.

"I want to help you." His voice brought her back, and she realized it was the whiteness of the room, the spears of sunlight coming in through the barred quiet room windows she had been feeling, and she was sweating now.

Dr. Burkert still kneeled. He shifted and tried to hold her eyes.

Lilly floated back into the dream trying to join the shrieking girl in the closet. But Dr. Burkert's savage journey through her was still real, and she lost the frame that separated her from him. He was reaching for her in the half-dream, and then in a flash he was beating her firmly with his hand. She heard her own cries. A plug from deep within her was pulled; a hole was exposed, as if she could feel her own breathing for the first time.

"What is it?" Dr. Burkert was asking, and Lilly realized he hadn't done a thing or heard her screams. It had all happened somewhere else. She came back into awareness, cooling. He went on, "It has been a very difficult morning for everyone. I spoke with Beverly, who was in the garden with you. She told me you were very agitated."

When Lilly jolted at the name, he drew back, hesitating in thought.

"Let's talk more about this later," he said. "I'll come back when you're feeling more able to let me."

₪

After Dr. Burkert left the quiet room, Lilly wanted to get up, unbearably anxious without his presence. She became certain that there was a beast in her belly. She was on the examining table inside the wild turbulence of her imagination again as her thoughts reentered the realm where the sublime fire waited. It was the wet orgasm she remembered now in the garden, how it had made her eyes close and then she had been lost behind a screen as if blind. Was there ever an end to the vortex and its diametrical pulls? Her eyes peered out into blackness now.

Lilly looked toward the quiet room window, burning to escape. She imagined a fall that would land her on the stones below. She tried to estimate the travel time between unscrewing the nuts that hinged the window, crushing her body through the small opening, and falling to her death. But the medicine was wrapping her thoughts into dull clouds; she was so tired she could not sustain the intensity. *Not tonight*, she told herself. *Not right now.* She could only surrender to the weight of her exhaustion.

Lilly sank into the mattress. It wasn't long before she closed her eyes and fell into her first deep sleep in days.

₪

Dr. Burkert came into the quiet room by late morning the next day.

"How are you?" he asked. "The nurses told me you slept last night. You seem calmer this morning."

"I didn't get enough sleep this past week. I was not myself."

"You haven't mentioned any feelings about Leonard's suicide."

"I was shocked. That's all. Everyone was." The ghosts had had their way with her, she thought, and now they were finished, their petering presences vanishing into her thick confusion. Late last night, unable to get back to sleep, Lilly had imagined a spirit as a cipher of matter, the weight of one teardrop, but it was gone now, she thought. She had fallen asleep again, and her body, rested now, seemed the only survivor of Leonard's and her father's fall, their death.

"Is that why you lost control?" Dr. Burkert moved closer to get to speak to her by the mattress. "From shock?"

"I told you," she said. "I wasn't sleeping. And I was frightened."

"But you told me you weren't sleeping before Leonard's suicide."

"Lots of things frighten me," she said, quickly. "It's nothing unusual."

"Were you frightened of Beverly? She told me she felt you were upset when you saw her there in the garden, and you were very anxious when she got near to you, to tell you you had to come back to the floor."

"She was the same nurse who examined me that first night I was admitted."

"But she wasn't able to examine you that night. You lost control like you did yesterday in your room after coming up from the garden."

"They took me up from the emergency room that night I was admitted, and I didn't even see my friend again. I was scared. I don't know what I told you."

"You said that you needed help. You seemed to be reacting to something in your body. It was terrifying to you. I told you there would be an examination, that a nurse would need to examine you to make sure there wasn't a physical cause you were describing. You lost control during the examination. I wonder if something like that happened with the same nurse Beverly in the garden."

"No, no. She doesn't have this effect on me. I was just very upset by everything, everything was very upsetting to me—I swallowed some pills the night I went to the emergency room." Lilly threw her head back, it felt heavy again. Then she watched him shift on the floor, but he didn't move closer to her.

"I think you are very upset by what happened in the garden with Beverly, and I understand you need to avoid that now," he said. "A patient here took his life yesterday morning, too. Did you know Leonard? The nurses have told me you and he talked together in the evenings."

"We knew each other for a very short time. There wasn't time to know him."

"I can understand how you may have felt devastated by what Leonard did. Did you want someone to make you feel safer after Leonard? After the morning?"

When her tears began, Dr. Burkert squatted beside her again. He smelled good and clean as a fresh bath towel.

"Getting close to people is hard for you," he said, gently. "And perhaps even harder with a woman."

For a second he understood, she thought. The room felt warmer.

She drew back, sucked in the wetness from her eyes. She started to speak, but then she stopped herself. "How long are you going to keep me in this room?"

"Not longer than I have to. I want you to feel more in control and hopefully understand why you lose control."

"Humiliation," she suddenly said, louder than she intended. "I feel humiliated. I'm just there so people can play with their ghosts, twist me any way they please into any meaning or non-meaning they please. Because I don't matter in the first place." It was the most she had said to him since she entered the hospital. She felt the looseness in her throat, words like a stream she couldn't help.

When she looked at him, his eyes were warm, resolved to stay in the room with her and listen.

She went on: "I vanish. One person or another tells me who I am and what I feel. One person or another tells me what to say and do. I thought if I tried hard enough I could end my banishment from myself. It felt like someone else had ordered this punishment."

"The punishment of—"

"Of not knowing who I was anymore."

"That's called depersonalization."

"Like my body," she said, now unable to stop herself. "My body was no longer familiar to me. But nothing was. I remember when I first felt I wasn't there in real space, maybe I had died with my father in the coma. Maybe I was brain-damaged, too. My mother was pushing at me, like she was entering me and I was disappearing. I can't really describe it."

"You're describing it very well."

She gathered herself up now. She had said too much, and she couldn't take it back.

But Dr. Burkert was looking intently at her, still in his same place. "That sounds terrifying," he said.

"So this means I have a severe diagnosis; my mother has damaged me."

"I'm not here to diagnose you. I'd like you to feel more comfortable and less damaged."

₪

Dr. Burkert came in the mornings for each of the days Lilly was kept in the quiet room.

The second morning she half-awoke, thinking that her father had died. But when she looked around the stark hospital room—the room was so vast. But then she was fully conscious, and she realized she was confined in a closed space. She listened to the clamber of patients moving through the halls, lining up with their coffee mugs in front of the dining room doors.

An odor halfway between the chemical smell of the highway below the barred window, and that of the tray of fried eggs on rye toast from her breakfast which she hadn't touched, hung in the white space.

A towel lay over the rim of the basin of water, now placed by a far wall. She remembered Caroline coming in very early this morning, around 6:30, and bringing the washbasin, the hand towels, and a tiny white bar of soap.

They could not risk taking her to the showers, Caroline explained (though in softer words), nor could the staff risk stripping her themselves, exposing her nakedness to another female nurse. Not until she felt better. They would let her wash herself here, using the basin of water. She had drifted off after breakfast was brought in. She only had a taste of the salty eggs before she went back to the mattress and fell into another deep sleep.

Now she heard a gardener's hose. It was 7:30, and she sniffed in wet dirt, flowerbed dirt. She got off the mattress and went to the window. Looking out, she saw the gardener in his green jumpsuit spraying the beds, the light purple flowers in the mud.

Caroline had wheeled in fresh clothes. Lilly thought that as soon as the morning nurse came to take her finished breakfast tray she would ask to be taken to the bathroom, which they would let her do, and ask if she could brush her teeth and her hair there. Then she left the window, washed and changed her clothes, trying to prepare herself for another session.

When she was finished, she looked around the padded room. The walls were still a shocking white but softer. The light delineating her silhouette on them had the gray intimacy of a Bedford morning inside her own bedroom when she was young. There was no noise from outside except for the muffled sounds of the highway below the barred window. The thick door was firmly shut.

By 8:30 a.m., from the portal-like window in the quiet room door, she observed Dr. Burkert as he talked to a slim woman, a young woman who was fragile and pretty. She wondered where he disappeared to during the day and night, how many patients he visited. Once she saw the retarded girl, Theresa, emerge from his office smiling, as if she'd had her first date with a man. Another time he walked an obese woman, with thickly coiffured hair and a kitchen apron strapped around her belly for no apparent reason, to her room after a session, guiding the woman through her imagined fears that a crowd of strangers might lunge from hidden corners of the corridor and attack her.

What was he thinking when his eyes plunged into them? Lilly wondered now.

Sometimes Lilly thought Dr. Burkert tried to break her down, into panic, into pieces. Suddenly her trust of him would crumble, and she saw a young, emotionally cold man who hadn't suffered, proffering himself to those who had suffered far too much—cruelly remote and superior. But now, the door was opened by an aide, and once again, Dr. Burkert arrived inside the room.

"How is it going?" Dr. Burkert asked.

"Did my mother call you?" she asked him.

"No. Why do you ask that?"

"I thought, maybe—sometimes I dream that my father is hurt, that he died. I think I was dreaming it last night. I think it's because of this room you put me in here. I would like to call my father, but I know my mother will be there. She takes over." She added, quickly, "Ever since his accident, I seem to be having this dream that he died."

"Because he can't stand up to your mother?"

"What?"

"He died because she takes over?"

"I didn't say that."

"Not directly. Tell me about the night of your father's accident."

"It was three years ago," Lilly said. "I already told you this."

"Is that when you first felt that you were vanishing, that your life would no longer be recognizable?"

"I don't know. I don't understand what you are asking me. I was alone in the house with my father—" She stopped for a second to check herself. "If you must know the details," she continued, restraining herself, "my mother went out that day to some garden club meeting. He was home because it was a Sunday. He slipped, but I didn't see anything. I didn't see him slip. I heard him fall down the stairs, a crashing sound."

"Yes?"

"He fell a second time into a coma. I don't want to talk about it."

"A second time?"

"I meant his second fall put him into a coma. He lay on the floor, and he was there so long, just lying there, I mean. When I heard my father out in the hall, I didn't go to him."

"Why?"

"I was upstairs, that's all.

"Hours later, my mother came back from the meeting and took over. She started yelling, she was hysterical, and crazy, and I rushed down, but I was frightened by her because she was talking really fast and she was so mad. I went right into the kitchen. I was sure he was there and just that they had a fight or something like that because she was so mad and yelling. But I saw him lying on the kitchen floor. He wasn't moving, but he was still breathing; his eyes were closed."

"Did your mother yell at you?"

"Yes. I didn't go down earlier to check on him. I should have realized his first fall was a stroke. She's not from this country."

"Yes, you told me that."

"She and my father, they didn't understand each other. She was unhappy, she wanted to go back to Israel."

"Were they separating?"

"She couldn't, not when he was sick like this."

"I see."

"I think I knew this." She stopped.

"Knew that she wouldn't leave him, or knew that she wouldn't leave you alone with your father in his condition?"

"She wouldn't leave me with him."

"She wanted to protect you?"

"Yes. But even before that she wanted to protect me. When I was a child, too. She didn't really have a good sense of how to do it. I mean, it felt like she wouldn't stop. She didn't live in her own country. And she wanted to leave."

"And in spite of everything, you needed her to stay."

"I don't want to talk about this. I told you. Why can't you just respect people here?"

He waited but Lilly said nothing more. "I do want to respect people, but I also need to help them," he said. "You're afraid to talk of needing your mother now. We'll stop now, and I'll be back this afternoon."

In the late afternoon, Dr. Burkert returned. "Let me ask you about your father," he continued as if there had been no break. "You visited your father in the hospital, when he was in the coma."

"Yes, I went." Lilly was feeling less drowsy, but restless. She wanted to get out of the quiet room now, and thought she should answer him. "We were together in the darkness."

"'In the darkness'?"

"I held his fingers. I talked to him by his bed, and we were together. We continued to speak when he went home. In the beginning, I stayed with him all the time. When I went to college, I came home almost every weekend for a long time and we spoke." Lilly broke off. Now she was saying too much.

"Did you ever talk about what had happened the night he had his strokes?"

"It didn't matter what I was saying. It was done. I couldn't change it. How could I? I couldn't change what happened to him. Don't you understand that?"

"But you sometimes worry that you might have."

"If I went down, if I got out of the water. I was upstairs, I was taking a bath. I just don't remember everything, that's all. It was a fucked-up night. My mother was leaving in two days. She was going away. I was taking a stupid bath and thinking about her leaving us."

"I see."

"If something happened, then she wouldn't leave, would she?" The fierceness in her voice startled her even more than her words. She was letting anger fly loose along with words. "So if something fucking terrible happened, she'd have to stay. And so I just didn't go down. I'm horrible, okay?"

"No, but I get the impression you've never spoken to anyone about this before?"

"Of course not. My mother was too freaked to come into his room downstairs. My mother left him there a lot alone. I came home to be with him, but all I could think about was running from there, the filthy room, his filthy sheets. I tried leaving her. I got a call in my apartment one day from the Bedford police that she had driven her car off a hill."

"On purpose?"

"I couldn't tell. She didn't tell me. She was hysterical."

"I see."

"I can't do this anymore," Lilly burst out. She was suddenly imagining him as feeling superior to her, looking down at her. He hadn't suffered—medical school all paid for, top grades, parents, what did he know about degradation and failure, being locked up, the self, a prison anyone could walk into? He talked as if people were pathetic for not managing themselves well, for simply not being able to survive anymore.

"I think you're afraid your mother or the nurse needs to punish you."

"No, I don't have fantasies like that!" she said, furious.

"What fantasies?"

"Please, will you leave me alone?" she said. "You put me in here! Just leave me."

He stepped back, away from her. "We'll pick this up tomorrow," Dr. Burkert said. "I'll come back in the morning."

₪

She fell back down on the mattress as Dr. Burkert shut the quiet room door. Her eyes stayed open against the white glare of the quiet room, and she was afraid suddenly that Dr. Burkert wouldn't return tomorrow. That she had scared or disgusted him away. That the warmth flowing in her system from his eyes would be taken from her. She imagined him handing the notes on her to some other doctor, and then she would be completely alone, lost into nothingness. She had told him too much. She felt the pull toward Dr. Burkert as a magnetic domination over her against which she had to fight, and then she clamped her eyes shut to escape it. She imagined herself in a far-off space, but then she was falling in midair and her body gave off a shriek that threw her out of this world, as if part of her had broken loose from corporeality, a state before disintegration, an instant where she could simply jump off the precipice of her being. Like a parachutist, her equipment would bloom into a massive white sail, and she would become found and lost at the same time. If it were psychosis, it was also where the bulb was supposed to take her, she thought, away from the reach of those who would undo her. And maybe it was madness after all, this place. She could accept that now.

After a while, she went to splash some of the water in the basin on her face. But then the soft crinkled cotton of her fresh T-shirt suddenly made her feel like a schoolgirl, and the feeling pricked at her like a bite from something underfoot and it kept on growing.

She felt pulled to lie back down on the mattress and then felt wetness like a vapor from some monstrous visitation enveloping her until she was moist all over. She struggled to hollow herself out, but the orgasm still came, a rich liquid warmth that made her feel that she was floating, gliding somehow. She let it pass out of her, without touching herself, and it rolled through her, lasting longer, and she felt its odd residue of trembling and pleasure.

She stood to eat her breakfast, feeling her hunger for the first time since she was brought to the quiet room.

₪

The next day, the quiet room walls hummed and murmured all morning with voices from the ward. Lilly looked out the small window on the quiet room to watch the activity in the hall as the day progressed. She watched Caroline instructing a handyman who held one of the hall lamps that another patient must have broken in a fit. She noticed a blonde, heavy woman in a blue hospital gown raise her hands to her tear-stained face. She couldn't quite make out the woman's words, but the woman was trembling and Caroline, standing sturdily, was explaining something to her after she turned from the handyman. Caroline's hairpins had fallen, and her hair bun was collapsed across her back—waxy-looking threads, disheveled but still able to hold their shape.

Lilly continued to watch the activity in the hall. Two people were talking, a man and a woman. The woman was wearing a black skirt and carrying an alligator handbag. Her lips were thin; the stripe of red lipstick looked like tape had been pulled over her lips. She was a visitor. Lilly knew by the way the woman was dressed, her spring raincoat still on. And she was carrying something in a bag for the man, who slowly peered into the bag and seemed to recognize its contents. *Clothes, things from his home*, Lilly thought. *The woman is his wife, or his sister.* The man's face tilted forward, and then she could see him well enough. He was taking out a pack of cigarettes, and now he held it out to the woman. When the woman shook her head at his offer, his eyes wandered over to the right of her shoulder and found Lilly's. He let his hand holding the pack of cigarettes slip down, and looked straight into the quiet room window. Then he had turned from Lilly and Lilly watched him, imagining him take hold of the woman and kiss her on those thin lips. A lover's kiss. Lilly didn't know whether she felt relief or loss, watching him.

₪

Dr. Burkert did not return that morning or early afternoon. After lunch, Lilly began to feel desperately empty again. She went to lie back down on the mattress and was pulled into a light nap. In her dream she heard her mother crying in the night, and Lilly went down the stairs to the living room. Helen asked her to keep her hand in her own. Helen lay back down on the couch under the painting of Old Jerusalem, and Lilly felt herself pulled near her mother. But she had become Beverly, the nurse, and her leg brushed against Lilly's skin and Lilly felt a sharp tingle in her thighs and then the room had darkened. Lilly pushed against the suffocation of her mother's need, which she still felt, but it was the eyes of the nurse that were looking into her and pressing, as if the eyes were her mother's lips.

Then someone else was rattling the doors in another dream waiting to enter. The image of the examining table came back into her awareness, and then Beverly was again bringing her into the invigorating caress. But she had felt an overwhelming sense of having lost herself. Everything within her was flowing and stirring, splitting her into pieces.

She awoke, sweating and terrified, as if a devouring ocean were rolling its waves toward her.

Her thighs and pubis had taken on the bruised tenderness of a woman who had sex. Then she began to cough, shivering. There was no blanket to warm her, and she no longer made an attempt to defend herself against the chill.

Lilly waited for the turbulence to pass, like a slow storm. A deepening doom clutched at her.

Lilly sat up and pressed her forehead against her knees, and her tears dripped onto the sheet. She felt helpless, sinking.

It was the first time since she came into the hospital that Lilly could not feel the bulb and felt no desire for her alchemy. She needed to be dead.

She closed her eyes and let herself drift, but it was a dreamless sleep, until again she slipped and was pulled back into the consuming ocean, sinking into a chasm, like buried bones.

When she awoke, she could not let herself fall back into sleep.

₪

"I was on call. I couldn't get here earlier. Are you all right?" Dr. Burkert asked when he arrived very late that night

He stared at her disheveled corner in the quiet room where she lay on the mattress, anxious, a thin blanket wrapped around her. She tried to push down her relief. But the blanket had slipped as she startled and sat up when he opened the door, and fallen into a mound around her waist.

"I'm sorry," she said to him now. "I wasn't able to stop."

"Stop? Do you mean your rage at me?"

"Yes," she lied. She had caught herself before stumbling, or exposing the distress of the last hours, she thought. But then she felt a beating heat again inside her.

"So you're still angry at me?"

"I don't want to be trapped here. You put me in here. I want to get out."

"You were put in the quiet room to help you calm down. This isn't a prison. As soon as you calm down, we'll move you back to your room."

She stood up but stepped back from him. She started to turn away and then, seeing the mattress and heap of blanket, felt the dream about the nurse arrest her again, and she stopped in mid-turn, as if suddenly drained of her sense of direction.

"What is it?" Dr. Burkert asked her.

When she faced him, she said, "I don't know . . . but . . . it's nothing. I'm not feeling well. That's all."

"You told me that when I spoke to you that first night you were admitted," he said, and slowly, cautiously, went on: "But something was happening to you, and you were terrified of it."

"It was a hallucination."

"Were you hallucinating when you looked at the mattress just now?"

"No, no. I just don't feel well, I told you." He was trying to unravel her on purpose, she thought. "I am losing myself. I told you, people make me into whatever they want. I disappear."

"These are dissociative states I think you might be trying to tell me about, brought on by the intrusions you experience in closeness. Closeness can be experienced as sexual and destructive. It can be overwhelming and terrifying."

Lilly felt alarmed and calmed by his words, bounding precipitously between panic and relief.

"I stopped by because I wanted to see how it was going for you in here, and if we can both consider moving you back to the hall. If you agree you still need the safety, I'd like you to spend the night here, and in the morning we can see about you leaving."

Lilly nodded and turned from him. She looked at the clock Caroline gave her, placed on the floor. It had stopped running, all out of batteries. It read 9:20 a.m. all day.

If I was staying in a hotel, I would always know the time and the day, she thought. *It's only in a hospital that time was an irrelevance.*

₪

The sunny morning made the outside world seem illuminated by a rich yellow light. Outside the quiet room window, the distant buildings looked bathed in early summer.

Waiting for Dr. Burkert, Lilly was already changed and washed. She ate her breakfast watching the sunlight as it grew, casting round yellow circles on the white wall.

But everything could fall apart, cracking into sudden rushes of scenes—the dirty sheets; her mother's reddening, tear-stained cheeks; her mother's brown, moist eyes and predatory passions.

As she waited for Dr. Burkert, she drifted into thoughts like a dream, imagining herself stranded at a train depot because she had missed her train. She was lugging around what was left of her possessions from the hospital which she had left to go home, and no one was helping her carry them. She then followed a man through a labyrinth of tracks—all to catch this train that the man said was running now from a different station to take her home. Her bags and suitcases were breaking in her arms. If she didn't catch the train, she would have nothing of her possessions, she thought, and she would be lost in endlessness.

When Dr. Burkert arrived in the late morning, a part of her sat beside him and a part of her sat across, far away from him with her eyes closed, stubborn and immobile, staring into his questions, mute. The part of her sitting beside Dr. Burkert felt like a nervous young woman, wondering who the other Lilly was and what brought her here.

"Are you feeling comfortable enough to go back to your room?" Dr. Burkert asked.

"I want to go back," she said.

"Does that mean you feel calmer?"

"I don't know what happened to me to make me come here."

"You said you felt you were vanishing—people, especially your mother, the nurse could make you feel obliterated and make you into whatever they wanted. Perhaps you feel a little more like yourself this morning."

"Yes, but I don't understand it all."

Later, that evening, in a session now in Dr. Burkert's office, Lilly, dressed back in jeans and her tee shirt continued: "I don't understand what you were telling me."

"I was explaining that feelings, even sexual feelings, can make us feel like someone is persecuting us," Dr. Burkert leaned forward in his chair across from her, as if there were a wall between them and she just had to put her ear to it and listen through it to hear him. "A little girl held too close by her mother," he went on, "may not be able to differentiate herself from the body of her mother, especially if she feels she is the exclusive object of her mother's desire, neither here nor there, just in a magnetic field which pulls and charges all the switches, emotional and sexual. It could be why that examination with the nurse your first night was so dangerous for you. And why I can be dangerous when you let me get close even you may need me to help you."

"I miss my father," she said, feeling herself push Dr. Burkert's words away now. "I wish my father were here right now."

"It's sad, your father does not come across as a protector after his brain damage, but sometimes even as another violator of boundaries."

"If I told you what I felt," she said. "You'd think I was crazy, I can't stand people knowing me—" She stopped. "It makes me mad and I feel like I'm fighting for my life. Something happens in my body that I can't handle. I can't stop it—, it's rape."

"I think closeness makes you feel obliterated," he said, carefully. "It's because you fight for your life against being annihilated that you become enraged at the people who are making you feel this way. Annihilation can be associated with orgasm, which can be a very confusing experience, sometimes it's called a ' little death'."

Lilly felt herself close to fracture and nearing a collapse into tears as she yielded to his words but she fought back from within. She gave into a long silence before she spoke. "Do we need to continue talking about all this?" She asked him.

"Yes," he answered. "This is very important."

When she looked at him, she thought she heard him say, "*Stay with me.*"

"What?" She asked.

"I said: stay with it," He answered. "And we'll work on this together."

₪

"Lilly, you know the rules." It was Caroline's voice Lilly heard, as Caroline ushered Lilly back into the eternity of the real, her first community meeting after the days in seclusion. Three days had already passed between the time Lilly was released from the quiet room this time.

"Find a seat," Caroline said to Lilly, who stood uncertainly by the far wall now. "I'm glad you feel ready to join us."

The hem of Caroline's summery shirt was loose, untucked, draping the nurse's cotton navy-blue skirt. The sniffling sounds of the seated patients had seemed too loud when Lilly was first released from the quiet room, as if the whole ward were crying.

Lilly settled into a stiff-backed chair. The sounds the patients made as they shuffled, coughed, and muttered seemed ordinary, just restlessness. She noticed the faces of a few new patients who had arrived while she was in the quiet room. But when she searched the faces, Lisa wasn't there.

A collection of clippings lay open on a lounge table next to the armchair where Lilly finally sat. She saw a headline and photo about Patty Hearst on the front page of the *New*

York Post. The headline read, "Patty Hearst Found at Another Crime Scene: Patty Hearst Now a Member of the Symbionese Army." This time she was at Mel's Sporting Goods Store in Englewood, California. From a van parked across the street from Mel's, shots were fired in the direction of the store. The shooter was identified as Patty Hearst, the newspaper article stated. Patty said that "out of the ashes" of the fire she "was reborn"—and "knew what she had to do next," the article read.

There were several copycat kidnappings, the newspaper reported. A male hairdresser in England staged a faux capture by left-wing blacks, and later emerged as a female, his hair womanly and long, two breasts formed by padding in a bra. He was wearing a soft chiffon dress and embracing a beautiful man with smooth ebony skin. A teenage girl faked a kidnapping and was found weeks later in Haight-Ashbury, pregnant and smiling.

No one could find Patty, the newspaper journalist said. There was no proof that it was Patty.

Patty Hearst has managed to escape her own life, Lilly thought, transmuting herself into another form, another self.

"Hi, Lilly," Louise said to Lilly now. "You look ravishing."

"Louise . . . ," Lilly said quietly, and she listened to the rhythm of her own voice. It calmed her against the hectic sneezing, turning, and fidgeting of the others. And soon, more vigorously, the motion of her legs crossing into the ordinary way she used to sit relaxed her fear.

"Are you well, my pet?" Louise teased.

Lilly nodded, smiling.

"Ladies, you know how these meetings are run," Caroline said. "This isn't a private conversation."

Lilly sighted the cabinet of records, magazines, and games. But of course she didn't see Leonard in his usual spot. They weren't talking about him now either. She rested her eyes on the floors, its familiar stains and marks. Some spilled backgammon die still lay where they had fallen. The floor hadn't yet been cleaned completely from the night, still soiled, so unlike the bald white of the quiet room's floor and its chalky finish, Lilly thought.

"Are people worried about when the new residents will come?" Caroline was asking the group. "It's going to be July soon."

"Where's Lisa?" someone was asking. "How come Lisa isn't here?"

"Lisa is seeing her family. She got a pass, and she is in Westport tonight," Caroline explained. "Are you feeling anxious about the July rotation of doctors?"

Lilly was certain Caroline was talking directly to her. But then she realized she had arrived late and the discussion had already started before she took her seat. Discharge dates moved up to accommodate the demands of the July rotation, the change in residents. Dr. Burkert had told Lilly that she would be discharged in about two weeks when he would be leaving the floor, and that he recommended they continue to work together in the outpatient department. She didn't want to think about it.

"Who will be my new doctor?" a female patient was asking.

"I want to leave, too," someone shouted.

The floor buzzed with the word "discharge" all that next week, and with the news of patients and to whom they would be assigned when the new residents arrived. Leonard's suicide still made the staff cautious. There were more staff aides in the corridor and more meetings; some morning meetings were held in the center lounge where the window had been repaired but the frame was still unpainted.

Chapter Ten

Wednesday, ten days before Lilly's discharge from the hospital, was another bright, sun-filled day. The hospital parking lot and the walkway were sheens of warm light as Lilly left on her first pass to her apartment in Little Italy. It wasn't an overnight pass yet, but she would have lunch with Jane and see their neighborhood for the first time since she was admitted. She was wondering what the warm outside sun would feel like on her, without anyone guarding her movements under it, when suddenly she saw her mother on the walkway.

"Hi, my darling," Helen said to Lilly as she approached, as if the chance encounter was almost expected. Both had halted as their eyes met.

"Don't be frightened, darling," Helen said softly. "I thought they told you. I have been coming to see Mrs. Levine, the social worker, for a few weeks. I came for our appointment today. This is why you see me here. She understands the grief I have been going through,"

"I'm glad," Lilly caught herself before she gave in to her body's shaking, to her shock. "I'm glad, Mom."

"Do you think we wanted this to happen to you?" Mrs. Weill spoke louder, as if in sudden desperation. She looked around the neo-Gothic establishment—the clipped gardens and spruce trees. "Your father doesn't understand what's happened to you," she said quickly. "But I want you to know, I do."

"I do—," Lilly started.

"I suffered a great deal, Lillian," Mrs. Weill went on. "You were in my belly once, you know. I feel all this."

Lilly flared in alarm. In her mind, Lilly shouted, *Mother, I am very angry*. When she was done thinking it, it was almost as good as if she had said it to Helen.

"The social worker knew right away I was a good mother. I didn't want so much to be on you. I had no choice."

"Yes," Lilly said, "I'm sure she did." She felt her mother's blindness to the boundaries, which separated them now as a sharp, lonely sorrow inside her. "Mom, has Daddy asked about me?"

"We must just accept what has happened to us," Helen said, as if she hadn't heard her. "We are in therapy now, and this is good." She held her head up high.

For moments, Lilly counted the leaves on the stone pavement. Then she thought her mother was weeping.

"Mom—" She looked into the puffy face. Helen's eyes looked moist, expanding in a ring of pain.

The warm waves of the June afternoon carried the grassy fragrances of the small plots of flowers that flanked the large neo-Gothic building and made it look like a keep-house in a sprawling diocese. Lilly remembered the place where the baptistery stood, the statues of Mother Mary and domed ceiling inside the cathedral.

"Mrs. Levine said you have trouble separating from me." Lilly knew, from the way her mother was talking, that her father hadn't asked about her, maybe he hadn't even noticed she was gone. *If he were thinking at all, it was about his Springbok notebook and the summer sparrows on the birch tree*, she thought. But her mother was here, in front of her.

"We can meet some time when you're 'ready,'" Helen told her.

"I would like that, Mom."

"Lilly," Helen said, raising her eyes again. "You know I never meant you any harm. You know that, don't you, sweetheart?"

₪

After her mother's visit, lying in her bed with her door shut, Lilly had pulled the white sheet up, under her chin, and imagined herself as an expanse of matter in a space between the stars and the planets. Lilly wasn't a "nothing" in this great vacancy, she thought. But as she lay there she felt a surge growing within her and she realized it was rage. Helen eyed Lilly in her dream this night. Helen is very tiny, and she is sitting in a big chair. She gives Lilly a look of exasperation, her head twitches away. But then her eyes come down hard on Lilly. Who was Lilly to touch and handle their love, and then throw away their precious union? Her mother's eyes were demanding.

₪

"Don't eat anything." The next day, sitting at a round breakfast table alone, a hungry Lilly was interrupted over a plate of scrambled eggs and rye toast by the aide named Stan. "Put the fork down, no food," he went on, "you're getting a blood test this morning." Her face fueled with fire. Lilly picked up the empty water glass as a fierce fury overtook her. "It's intolerable, here, " she started as Stan was pulling the plate of food away, out from under her. But then, filling with rage, she was aiming the glass at the window. She suddenly felt Caroline yanking the glass from her upraised hand, backing Stan away from her shouts: "Let her get control herself, Stan, everyone stop staring!"

Then: " Lilly, please," Caroline said and Lilly unclenched the glass as Caroline grabbed it. Just as quickly, Lilly bolted from the dining room. She ran down the corridor as other patients moved to the dining room exit and stared at her. Hushed and startled again by the sudden rages which it seemed would once again explode in the quiet Lilly, who had rarely said a word to anyone, hazy and inaccessible for all these weeks. Always watching others, agreeable, listening. The rages came like surges, as though she were possessed.

Now Lilly slammed her bedroom door shut, kicked it from the other side, thinking the thrust hard enough to break the wood.

"But did she throw anything?" she heard Dr. Burkert suddenly ask outside her door.

"No, no." It was Caroline who answered Dr. Burkert, and Lilly realized Caroline had called him. The door was still intact when Lilly opened it to let Dr. Burkert inside her room.

Dr. Burkert stood in Lilly's bedroom moments later, his left elbow leaning against the top of her bureau's flat top, and he watched Lilly as she started breathing deeply and slowly to calm herself.

She made herself sit silently in the desk chair, and she breathed and breathed until her body stopped shaking.

Then she had started to cry feverishly, and with such pain that she sounded as if she had swallowed broken glass. She sounded as if she could never come back.

He waited. Then, "Come to my office," he said.

She followed him down the corridor, *a person made of gasps of air*, she thought.

₪

"I understand you saw your mother yesterday." Dr. Burkert said as Lilly sat in her usual chair.

"No," she said. "Not saw, I ran into her."

"This morning she called me to tell me she hoped we could have a family session, she said she would be able to bring your father, you had asked about him. How would you feel about that?"

Lilly hesitated, her breathing had eased but now she heard the clack-clack-clack of the big fan on the ceiling over his desk, it was noisily turning but why hadn't she heard it when she first walked in. She felt the wind it made on her legs, he seemed to have aimed it at her, before she walked in, and it blew at her lap.

"We were talking about you leaving the hospital in ten days? Are you in control? Will you be ready?"

"Can I ask you to please turn that thing off," she said.

"The fan?"

"Yes," she pointed at the fan.

"Okay, if you're uncomfortable." Dr. Burkert stood, his finger pressed on the red square button that controlled the offending object.

She moved in her seat. "You're talking about discharging me. I'm just nervous, that's all."

"Did seeing your mother have something to do with how angry you're feeling this morning?"

"I'm not leaving the hospital to be with my mother," she said.

"Your mother was very overwhelmed herself when she spoke with me."

"I'm guilty," Lilly said. "I destroyed her life."

His hand carved a space in the air, then his fingers closed in on his own palm. "Destroyed her life—how?"

She knew when she looked at him—if only for an instant this time—that beneath her storm and the rage, there was still something else beckoning where the bulb had made a place within the confusion that swam inside her, and she felt herself reaching for the familiar feeling of escape where she would evaporate, flow invisibly as a stream of breath beyond what was there. But it didn't happen this time, her vanishing. She felt, instead, the weight of her own unbroken will. "I don't want a family session," she said firmly.

Lilly was certain that, when he looked at her waiting for her to answer, he had taken her silence for the opposite of what it meant, as a compliance with what he was saying. "Fair enough," he said. "I'm glad you feel the work we are going to do together will help you feel a distance from her. Safe. We have a lot to prepare for before you leave." When a commotion started outside his office, he rose from his desk, distracted.

"We'll continue this later," he said. And then she was sure he couldn't have known that she, just at that moment, wanted to run away from everything he had been planning for her.

₪

That was the day, during visiting hours, when, with so much activity in other parts of the ward, the door was loosely guarded by the staff. Lilly watched doors to the outside hall and elevators open and close as a nurse let various visitors onto the ward. But then she found herself trying to control her impulse to throw something, to break a window. Why did she want to do such a thing? She prodded herself, imagining Dr. Burkert standing there in the doorway. Would he stand and stare at her and wonder how far she would go?

Was he rescuing her from her mother only to put her under *his* control?

Suddenly, one of the nurses opened the door to the outside elevator vestibule to let out a waiting family. The nurse was distracted by another visitor, and Lilly lurched through the doorway. The door closed behind her. Then she was feeling the cool, metallic air outside the ward in the small vestibule before the elevators. The elevator came, the visitors entered, she remained behind and heard the elevator door clack shut, leaving her alone in the vestibule. It felt unbearably strange to be alone, of her own volition, without any permission from staff for the first time in over eight weeks.

Run. Hail a taxi, Lilly suddenly thought. *Get to Little Italy. Watch the night fall over the bridge.* She would pay the fare and jump out. She would escape Dr. Burkert and his "preparations." *Control the ending of all this, instead of him*, she thought. She remembered how much she had missed the balcony in the evenings at Elizabeth Street. Hadn't she often stood on her apartment's balcony overlooking the pavement where the men came from the Salvation Army building across the street, exiting with only a bag of belongings, but no money, fresh faces, skin rashes that were raw from scrubbings in the shelter? She had watched them nuzzle together on the Bowery, free until the next time they knocked at that door. She had stood on that balcony a thousand times, awestruck at the ease with which each of those men had, without shame, continued his fecund and anonymous wanderings, thinking, *It could never be me.*

She paced restlessly now in these first few moments inside her own space. But then she was filling with an anxiety deeper than she had ever felt. She conjured the sound of Dr. Burkert's voice. He would be angry if she discovered her here, she thought, remembering how much of a disciplinarian he was when she fought him to get loose from his hold the days in the seclusion room, his words like waves of water slapping her. Suddenly, she felt the life in her sex aroused by the dread of being caught by him, and by the fear of what would happen to her if he found her. She trembled. She heard the elevators, but they were below her, all the way down near the lobby. She had but a few moments before the elevator would ascend again, and open, and possibly halt at her floor. Caroline, an aide, or another nurse could emerge from the locked door behind her. She implored and dreaded that the elevators would arrive, open, and free her from feeling this dreadful pleasure.

But Lilly reached and touched herself under her waist-
band. She knew she had seconds before a door would open,
and someone would enter and take it all away from her again.
Daring everything, she felt for the life in her sex. Then it was as
if she were pulled down to a blade. Her skin had turned into a
nightgown, she was crepe, and she slid across Dr. Burkert in her
fantasy. She imagined his penis and he was there, she control-
ling him. What pact with the ghosts, the fallen, and those who
would dominate and beat her had she traded for this phantom
of equal danger? Then, what could she possibly do about it now?
She asked herself, but then she knew this was her turning point,
swelling up inside her like a siren. On the edge of her fantasy,
she approached the familiar annihilation, but it was pure and
she felt good. She was still whole when her body ejected an
orgasm with the logic of a flower. And then nothing hurt inside
her but pleasure.

She let the orgasm run through her, as her own genesis.
Was she crazy? Who was she?

She wouldn't have a weighty newspaper trial like Leonard
for her crimes, the whole city hunting for a drug-eyed gradu-
ate student who accidentally went insane out of confusion and
violence. Or be like Patty Hearst, holding a gun in her tender
hands. Lilly wouldn't be her father either, falling accidentally
down a stairway, profound and snarled as a snake in one's heart.
She would not be executed or humiliated by cold dominators.
She knew it was Dr. Burkert, the fantasy of him—that had
brought her climax to its blossoming—but she didn't care. Lilly
threw her head back; it felt heavy again. But hadn't she been
courageous? She had unfolded herself, survived by riding on
shooting stars. The doctor would never love her in return. Nor
care for her beyond the fence put between them by their real
functions, but even that felt good. She had used him for her
own purposes.

Lilly stood alone out in the hallway for the few minutes it took for the elevator to ascend past her floor, not stopping.

She was undiscovered.

Lilly waited and then there was an opening. One of the nurses turned to answer a guest's question and the visitor door was open.

By her own accord, by her decision alone, Lilly quietly stepped back onto the ward.

Chapter Eleven

LILLY'S NOTEBOOK:

Entries From My Room on the Fifth Floor at Payne Whitney Psychiatric Hospital July 1-13, 1974.

Historical Positioning:

ST. FRANCIS AND THE LEPER. The First Recorded Incident of the Therapy Called "The Laying On Of Hands", 1200 AD.

The Brethren were working in the leper infirmary. St. Francis was near, at a convent in the village. There was a leper inside the hospital said to be possessed by the Devil. They called her "The Perverse One". The leper spat food back at those who served her. She wouldn't let anything—words or nourishment—enter her body. She pranced about, haughty, pinching her lips closed. And she clipped her nose shut with a wooden pin so she wouldn't smell herself. She tore the clothes off that the Brethren tried to dress her in, demanding to stay in her own clothing though the cloth was corroded with leprosy. None of their oils or powders could heal her diseased skin. None of their sympathies subdued her raging.

They said the imprint of the Devil's claw was on some secret part of her body. And when she cried—they said it was because that spot was tingling painfully—the Devil was calling her to a Sabbath. All day she blasphemed. Against the Holy Mother. Against the Brethren. Against the other lepers. And worst—against her own hated self.

After weeks, her skin gave off a stench so foul, the Brethren had to remove her from the rest of the leper community. They isolated her in a barren room. They took the wooden pin off her nose, forcing her to smell herself and stew in her own filthy odors. She cried harder, more urgently, when the spot tingled, because the room was nailed shut at every opening. There was no way to get out and ride the Devil's goat when it came to the barred window to take her to the Sabbath.

"Her skin stinks like that," the Brethren said, "because the Devil's juices are boiling inside it. If we don't keep her locked up they'll leak out all over the community."

The Brethren hoped the room could hold the escaping vapors. But, fearing that it wouldn't, they asked St. Francis to come.

St. Francis entered the seclusion room where the leper was being kept. His robe was white and clean. And his hands were flawless and smooth as the robe. The leper backed away from him, warning: "If you come too close, my Devil Juices are going to spill out all over you and destroy that robe of yours."

St Francis held out his hands, unafraid of the leper's skin as it filled the air with vapors from the Devil's bowels. "I don't believe in "Saints," the leper snapped. "Get your hands away or the Devil juices are going to burn them like acid and make leprosy grow on them after."

St. Francis's hands stayed outstretched. One, sturdy and determined, held a sponge. "You couldn't wash me," the leper said. "They've all tried to wash me. I can't be washed." St. Francis ordered water to be brought and heated with sweet-smelling herbs. He told the Brethren to strip the leper naked. Once she was exposed, the leper's fighting arrogance disappeared. And the shame of the disease that covered her body made her freeze like hard metal in their hands. As the Brethren poured the water, St. Francis stroked and bathed the leper.

Very soon, the nodules of leprosy and the layers of soil vanished from the leper's body. Underneath was new skin, so raw only St. Francis' skilled hands knew how to handle it. Vulnerable to every sensation, no matter how slight, the new skin had to be encased in a special gel-like substance and wrapped in soft cloths. The leper herself wasn't allowed to touch it. Its new veins and sensitive fibers could easily burst out bleeding beyond control if disturbed by unknowing hands.

The Brethren bound the leper's hands behind her back, saying that they must protect her from her own chance itches should her hands touch the new skin by mistake in her sleep. Though the torment of her other life and the painful tingle from the Devil's imprint were both gone now, the leper was a stranger to her own skin. She was helpless in the hands of St. Francis, dependent on the Brethren for feeding and dressing. The love she had for them, there because she was ignorant of her own flesh, brought her more shame than the leprosy they had cured."

When Lilly stopped reading what she had written the last week, she felt a feeling of extraordinary lightness. For hours in the hospital, Lilly had hardly done anything else but write, as if she had just discovered it.

The myriad reasons for her hospital stay seemed to her like a soap opera sometimes: her father's accident on the stairs, the two years of caring for him, then the phantom bulb, the "psychosis", the melodramatic and hysterical language inside her head. The world was cloudier now that the bulb,— the delusion, —had vanished into her own history, but the world was closer to her, too.

Picking up her pen in her room now, Lilly continued her "notes."

Notes.

1. The remedy for all the disorders of the soul, said Plato, is the same: "the use of certain charms'. These charms are 'fair words' and 'beautiful reasons".

2. FROM: *The Art of Alchemy*, by Maurice Aniane: *"Finally, it may be that alchemists knew of certain erotic "techniques" similar to those of Tantrism and intended to awaken the energy of sex without allowing it to be wasted in unwanted orgasm."*

3. In the 17th century, alchemy was discredited by Robert Boyle,and the entire Royal Society of London. (Though Isaac Newton himself secretly admitted he used alchemical theory for his own scientific inquiries and experiments.) The penalty for the practice of alchemy was death. Because of the process in alchemy which involved multiplication of a small gold particle into large pounds of gold for profit, alchemy was suspected as a fraudulent science to produce illegal gain."

₪

The morning of Lilly's discharge, Lilly awoke and the fine haze that usually veiled her awakening gradually dispersed. Lilly pulled the chain of the reading lamp. The room was still dark but a blade of sunlight struck the clothes she had placed on the brown faux leather armchair last night. She startled at how neatly she had arranged her blue jeans, the red Bloomingdale's leather-strapped sandals with giant cork soles— the style she had watched the nurses wear to work all month. Under the jeans, she had harbored a light button-down blouse that wasn't a Tee shirt, but had "Made in Italy" on its silky label, along with "only to be hand-washed. Do not put in the washing machine or dryer".

Helen did not come to the ward to visit. Dr. Burkert had let Lilly decide when and how she would see her mother again. Lilly could have run back into her madness, she thought now, until she reached a place where she would not be able to choose any more. But she had only touched real madness, she thought now, at the rim, she had eluded its seduction down into some irreversible and final absorption and scattering, into extinction. She was lucky, and that was enough for now. She was lucky, and she was a fighter, she reassured herself.

She glanced up into the mirror above her bureau. In the reflection she saw herself, a pale but intense figure.

Beside the stubby armchair legs, the portion of Jane's baked walnut bread Lilly hadn't been able to finish last night scented a grocery bag. Dropping it into the bag, she had later lain wide-awake until 4 am. She now figured she had finally dozed off and caught two hours of sleep. It was six-thirty by the electric clock on the bureau. She must get dressed. She needed to hold on to the self she was feeling. In the night she had worried about the bulb, but for now, it wasn't on her mind.

From the view outside the window, she could not see the ramp, or the outpatient clinic Dr. Burkert had so carefully ex-plained to her. She would put the schedule up on the refrigera-tor door once she got to the apartment in Little Italy. Jane had said she would be there by three this afternoon; they could go to a movie "or something".

Wisps of morning cloud twirled up over the parking lots, appearing as smoke, but they were illusory and deceptive, she knew, only the July air teasing with its licks of vapors before a beating heat would fall down on all who walked below. But then she was remembering the college gardener's sprinkler on the blueberry bushes at Sarah Lawrence in summer, and how the berries became warm and sweet. She had picked them once and washed them in the lavatory in the back of the Pub, it was the one of few times college had felt good to her. She was caught now between this world of patients and the hospital—--which no longer wanted much to do with her—- and the world outside, where she didn't want to vanish. She felt herself forced between the hospital's protection and the most essential of human challenges, that of merely moving forward, of setting some inner gears and moving through fragility.

How they did all survive? She wondered. All her alchemists, all her fellow patients? Did they survive? Will she? She could see a whole tribe of people, connoisseurs of isolation and loneliness and invisibility to which she belonged.

Lilly rejected the idea of checking through all her bags again, to make sure she had everything, or of opening and shutting the drawers, or poking at the empty hangers that now lay empty-shouldered, gray-black, hard wire on a pole strewed across the top of the closet.

She needed to gather up all her other things, glancing for the last time at the armchair, the desk, the metal frame of the bed with its four crowned posts, and the screened window where the morning light shimmered.

She whisked her notebook up off the bureau, and glimpsed at the newest swiftly written, almost breathless sentence. She had written down the feelings of yesterday, and further back. She had tried to recapture experiences she'd had in the hospital; rolling currents of feelings put into words which were spurts and splashes on the pages now of a notebook she bought from the hospital canteen weeks ago, but couldn't start filling until she left the quiet room. The time she threw the lamp in her room... Leonard's first talking to her, the night she awoke to the men singing him a birthday song, the face and hands of Beverly and the dreams of beatings and examining tables. Turning the pages, she saw again how she had filled the last days of her hospital stays with descriptions of the other patients, episodes she had felt compelled to write about on the hall. Pages, both random and ordered by a deeper place inside her than she knew existed now, the engine of her madness and her health intermixing, begging for consolidation—the night of her father's accident on the stairs, the night which made little sense but became a starting point for all the sense yet to come to her, Helen, and Helen's connection to everything else. Each page was like a room of many empty naked beds and trembling shadows, but Lilly was in the heart of a circle of light, shrinking back a little from the glare. And Dr. Burkert, the slender man was only a wind of maleness, like a breeze, the weather inside her damp and motionless.

Now Lilly began collecting all her sheets of writing up into a kind of file to put below her other belongings in the bags with the notebook.

"*Elsewhere,*" she read from the chapter of the alchemy text she had found again in a shopping bag Jane brought her at the beginning of her hospital stay, called: THE OPERATION TO THE PHILOSOPHER'S STONE, "*...the operations are there to baffle the vulgar, and reckon with the alchemist... the stages of the Great Work can appear to the alchemist as symbols, shadow, and paroxysms like the philosophic trees that spring from the phalluses of the androgens, from Saturn and Venus.*"

Lilly remembered it was Helen who gave her the first notebook. It was somewhere in the closet inside her old bedroom in Bedford, buried like an abortion under a pile of outgrown clothes. She had bound it in some scraps of leather from her mother's bookbinding table, and on the cover, in her childish scrawl, written: *I would like to write novels someday and I like poems too.*

She looked at her appointment schedule for next week. Dr. Burkert, Tuesday, Wednesday, Thursday. He would be back, she thought, thinking of him last evening in her room, telling her where the outpatient department was sheltered under a brownstone overhead. "Past the parking lot," he had explained. "You go down a ramp." Lilly perused the form he had brought in for her to sign. She suddenly wanted to see, too, his signature beside hers, as if to convince herself that something—an insight, a feeling, an idea— he had showed her in the white room, or in his office, could cause equilibrium enough for her walk out of the hospital today, into the summer morning. She read:

> White female
> Age: 22
> Prognosis: Good
> Date released: July 20, 1974
> Reason given for discharge:
> No longer a danger to herself.